George Body

The activities of the ascended Lord

Adapted by permission, from instructions given Rev. George Body, M.A.D.D.

George Body

The activities of the ascended Lord
Adapted by permission, from instructions given Rev. George Body, M.A.D.D.

ISBN/EAN: 9783741189555

Manufactured in Europe, USA, Canada, Australia, Japa

Cover: Foto ©Andreas Hilbeck / pixelio.de

Manufactured and distributed by brebook publishing software
(www.brebook.com)

George Body

The activities of the ascended Lord

THE ACTIVITIES

OF

THE ASCENDED LORD.

ADAPTED BY PERMISSION, FROM INSTRUCTIONS GIVEN

BY THE

REV. GEORGE BODY, M.A. D.D.

CANON OF DURHAM.

SECOND EDITION.

LONDON:

WELLS GARDNER, DARTON & CO.,

3, PATERNOSTER BUILDINGS, E.C.,

AND 44, VICTORIA STREET, S.W.

Preface.

THESE Readings on the Ascended Life of our LORD have been arranged on a plan similar to that of the volume published two years ago under the title of "The Appearances of the Risen Lord;" and it is owing to the kindly expressed assurances that have reached me of the value of that book that I have been encouraged to put forth the present one.

Once more my thanks are due to Canon Body for the unstinted generosity with which he has allowed me to make free use of my notes of his Instructions, and once more I desire to add that he is in no way responsible for the publication of this volume.

I am indebted to the Bishop of Lichfield for allowing me to quote part of his hymn on the Holy Communion, and to the Compilers of "Hymns, Ancient and Modern," for the use of No. 316 in their Hymnal.

May GOD, of HIS great kindness, grant that the deeper teaching of the Ascended Life of JESUS may bring deeper blessing to the souls whom HE has prepared to receive it.

S. F. L. S.

Easter, 1891.

Contents.

First Reading.

S. LUKE xxiv. 50, 51; ACTS i. 6–9; PSALM xviii. 10, 12 (P. B. V.).

AND He led them out as far as to Bethany, and He lifted up His Hands, and blessed them. And it came to pass, while He blessed them, He was parted from them, and carried up into Heaven.

When they therefore were come together, they asked of Him, saying, LORD, wilt Thou at this time restore again the Kingdom to Israel? And He said unto them, It is not for you to know the times or the seasons, which the FATHER hath put in His own power. But ye shall receive power after that the HOLY GHOST is come upon you : and ye shall be witnesses unto Me, both in Jerusalem, and in all Judea, and in Samaria, and unto the uttermost part of the earth. And when He had spoken these things, while they beheld, He was taken up ; and a cloud received Him out of their sight.

He rode upon the Cherubims and did fly : He came flying upon the wings of the wind. At the brightness of His Presence His clouds removed.

I.

THE REVELATION OF THE DESTINY OF HUMANITY.

THERE are many aspects under which the Christian Life is set before us in the Bible. It is sometimes spoken of as " Walking with GOD,"—that is, as a life of realized communion with an ever-present, watching, sustaining FATHER. Again, it is called " Abiding in CHRIST,"—a phrase which implies not merely a life lived in the grateful remembrance of benefits once received, or in loyal obedience to great teaching once given, but in continual communion with a Living LORD, that LORD Who is living His Life as an ascended life since He has " passed into the Heavens." The subject we are about to consider may therefore be defined as Christian Life lived in union with the Ascended JESUS CHRIST.

Let us begin by taking for our contemplation to-day the vision of the Ascension itself, and observe the light which is cast by it on the great mystery of our own life. And first, it is most important for us to understand clearly and distinctly what the Ascension of JESUS CHRIST really is. The Ascension of JESUS CHRIST is a historical fact. Just as truly as Calvary was the scene of the great historical event of the

Crucifixion, so truly were the heights of Olivet the scene of the great historical event of the Ascension; just as truly as, in His assumed Humanity, He died on Calvary, and rose again from the tomb of Joseph of Arimathea, where He had slept His mysterious sleep, so truly on Olivet did our LORD, in His assumed Humanity, pass from earth to Heaven.

"He led them out as far as to Bethany, and lifted up His Hands and blessed them; and as He blessed them, He was parted from them, and carried up into Heaven" (S. Luke xxiv. 50, 51.) Now, the Ascension of JESUS CHRIST is continually spoken of as though it were His return to conditions of being which He had temporarily resigned for the purpose of His redeeming work, and which, when that work had been accomplished, were again resumed. It has been maintained that our LORD's heavenly life was really laid aside when He assumed the conditions of human life. But, as a matter of fact, the truth is this: our LORD never did cease to live His heavenly life,—He did not live His creaturely life by ceasing to live as the Creator,—He did not become the Child of Mary and tabernacle in the Virgin's Womb by ceasing to be in the Bosom of the FATHER. Because the heavenly life of our LORD is *essential*, while His human life is *accidental*, it is inconceivable that our LORD ever ceased for one moment to live His life as the Eternal Son of GOD. He speaks of Himself even when on earth as being in Heaven: "No man hath ascended up to Heaven, but He that came down from Heaven, even the Son of Man Which is in Heaven" (S. John iii. 13); and S. John proclaims the same truth when, in the

introduction to his Gospel, he says : "No man hath
seen GOD at any time ; the Only-Begotten Son Which
is in the Bosom of the FATHER, He hath declared
Him" (S. John i. 18). Our LORD's Ascension, therefore, could not be His return to suspended conditions
of divine life, because those conditions of divine life
never for one moment knew suspense. No ; the
Ascension of JESUS CHRIST is the first entrance into
Heaven of Humanity in the fulness of glory and power.
Through the operation of the HOLY GHOST the Eternal
Son took unto Himself all the constituent parts of
our human nature. He took that nature under the
conditions of infancy, and held it through all its
stages. The infant became the boy, the boy became
the youth, the youth grew into manhood, as we do ;
and He died the death we die, and slept the sleep we
sleep in the grave, and rose from the tomb, resuming
the same human nature under glorified conditions.
And then, when the forty days were passed, He
carried it up to His glorious Home above ; in it He
passed through rank after rank of the angelic host,
who thronged about Him as He went up,—those who
closed in after Him and "received Him out of the
sight" of His disciples, crying (in the jubilant language of the 24th Psalm) to the bands who awaited
His approach: "Lift up your heads, O ye gates,
and be ye lift up, ye everlasting doors, and the King
of Glory shall come in !" and answering the eager
response, "Who is the King of Glory?" by the tri-
umphant announcement, " Even the LORD of Hosts,
He is the King of Glory !" In that human nature
He passed on His majestic way till "Angels and

Archangels and all the Company of Heaven" were left behind, till (in the mysterious language of the Bible) He came to the very Presence Chamber of Him Who yet has no Presence Chamber; and there crowned with everlasting glory, He, the Child of Mary, the Son of Man, is, in His assumed Humanity, throned for ever at the Right Hand of the Majesty on high.

The Ascension of JESUS CHRIST, then, restores mankind to its abiding state. We find ourselves sometimes asking, "Why did GOD create man? What is man's end, his abiding state?" And we find the answer to this question in the Ascension of JESUS CHRIST. In His Humanity we can trace the whole course of human life. As CHRIST from the Manger of Bethlehem passed to the Presence Chamber of Heaven, there to be throned at the Right Hand of GOD, so you and I are called into being to find the true end of our being in the Presence of GOD.

This is the first great light that flashes across our path as we consider what the Ascension of JESUS CHRIST is in relation to man. If we are really to decipher the laws of human life, we must consider that life not under transitory but under abiding conditions. Confessedly, it is lived here under transitory conditions,—and we have to remember that, since man's life on earth is not his true state, the ideal of his existence can never here be fully realised; for man was created for eternity, not for time; for Heaven, not for earth. I know that there lives in Heaven One not separated by any insuperable barrier from His fellows in the race, but their Forerunner,—

One in Whom human life is lived under its true conditions, in Whom humanity has attained the true end of its being,—and I know that, as He ascended, I shall ascend, and with Him continually dwell.

Having thus placed before my mind the vision of the Lord's Ascension, I can see in it, as His pure Humanity rises from earth to Heaven and rests at GOD's Right Hand, the revelation to myself of the end of my being. But with this revelation there comes before the mind the connection existing between the Celestial life above and the terrestrial life lived here on earth. For the Ascension is not an isolated fact; it is a fact led up to by those of a life on earth; and we have to recognize this truth: that JESUS merited His resurrection, His ascension, His perpetual glory, by the life He lived and the death He died upon earth. Our LORD comes and takes our nature upon Him that He may be the " Priest seated upon His Throne " (Zech. vi. 12), the King-Priest of humanity; but if He is to be this Priestly King of the race of mankind, and to bring the race over which He rules to the heights of the heavenly life, He must merit that Priesthood and that Kingdom by the obedience of His perfect life and His atoning death. It is by His merits in His assumed Humanity that JESUS won for us the glories of the heavenly life.

Thus, by the fact of His Ascension the LORD reveals to us our earthly life under two aspects. First, He teaches us that earthly life is the sphere of merit —that we have to merit here our future glory. Do not think that by this I mean that we can of ourselves

merit anything apart from the grace of GOD.   No; all
power to merit anything is simply the result of GOD's
grace.   The grace of God must inspire us, aid us,
remove our imperfections,—His grace alone can
enable us to merit glory; but grace must be re-
sponded to.   "Work out your own salvation," says
S. Paul, "for it is GOD that worketh in you" (Phil
ii. 12, 13).   Grace calls; I respond.   Grace enables;
I act.   But if I thus respond, if I thus act, I see
no presumption in believing that I shall then obtain
the promised reward,—that by doing what He would
have me do, and bearing what He would have me
bear, I may merit the reward which He, of His free
grace, promises.   Is it not so?   What does our
LORD teach us in the parable of the Sheep and
the Goats?   "Come, ye blessed of My FATHER,
inherit the Kingdom prepared for you from the
foundation of the world."   Why?   "Because, in the
power of grace, ye have fulfilled the impulses of
charity, and have done deeds according to My Will."
"He that is faithful in that which is least, is faithful
also in much; and he that is unjust in the least, is
unjust also in much.   If therefore ye have not been
faithful in the unrighteous mammon, who will commit
to your trust the true riches?" (S. Luke xvi. 10, 11).
We see, then, that we are set here on earth in the first
place for this purpose : that, treading in the footsteps
of JESUS CHRIST by active obedience, and following
the example of His patience by passive obedience, we
may merit that which He has won for us, even the
ascended life.

But there is another aspect under which our life

here is presented to us in the light of the Ascension. Our LORD reveals it to us not only as the sphere of merit, but, secondly, as the school for Eternity. Why is a boy sent to school? That he may be trained to meet the responsibilities of life. When at school he cannot understand the necessity of the discipline, and perhaps he looks upon it as hard,—but the parents know that if they weakly yielded to his reluctance, the time would come when, as a man, he would blame their foolish indulgence as the cause of his unfitness for the serious business of life. And the only thing the boy can do in the meantime is to have confidence in his parents and in his master, and to bear as best he can all that is fretting and perplexing to him, trusting in their care for his future welfare. Now, it is under just such conditions that we live here and now. As our LORD could only reach His Ascended Life after the wounds had been graven in His sacred Hands and His Heart had been broken on the Cross, so we can only become fitted for our ascended life through the daily discipline of our life on earth. For the first condition of blessedness in the ascended life is the development of character to GOD's ideal, and this development can only be accomplished by means of the educating discipline of daily life, of our training in the school of GOD.

Believe me, nothing comes to us by chance. Every duty is GOD-assigned, every trial is GOD-sent, every temptation is GOD-permitted. It is all part of GOD's loving discipline, sent to heal what needs healing in us, to develop that which needs developing, to make us what He would have us to be, beautiful with the

beauty of the Christ-like character. And as I lie
low in meditation before the Ascended One, and
see that—

> " Those dear tokens of His Passion
>   Still His dazzling Body wears,"

I realize that it is indeed the Crucified One Who is
enthroned, and from His Wounds I learn that the
way to the Throne is the way of the Cross.

These are the primary thoughts with which we
must enter upon our present subject of meditation.
First, we have to face the great historical fact of the
Ascension of JESUS CHRIST, and to see in it the revelation of the true end of man's being,—Heaven our
Home, GOD our End. Secondly, we recognize in the
life of JESUS CHRIST on earth before His Ascension
the revelation of the conditions of our attaining that
appointed end. Thirdly, we learn that through the
discipline of life in time we merit eternity, and that
in the school of time we are trained for eternity.

And what is the practical outcome of these thoughts?
Surely they lead us to self-oblation. Never mind how
hard and trying the conditions of your life on earth
may be,—'tis but for a little while, and the darkness is
GOD-sent. Meet your trials, laying hold with a firm
faith on this truth : GOD created me for eternal union
with Himself; Heaven is my home, life in the Presence
of GOD is the end for which I am called into being ;
I am placed here but for a little while, to live on earth
a life of union with JESUS, and to imitate His obedience, in order that here I may merit eternal glory,
and here be educated for my eternal home. Welcome,

then, sorrow, cares, soul-darkness! They are but the loving discipline whereby my GOD trains me for the heavenly life,—they are but a share in that cup of which the Ascended One drank, of the Baptism wherewith He was baptized!

Second Reading.

ACTS vii. 55, 56, 59, 60.

BUT he, being full of the HOLY GHOST, looked up stedfastly into Heaven, and saw the glory of GOD, and JESUS
standing on the Right Hand of GOD, and said, Behold, I
see the Heavens opened, and the Son of Man standing
on the Right Hand of GOD. And they stoned Stephen,
calling upon GOD, and saying, LORD JESUS, receive my
spirit. And he kneeled down, and cried with a loud
voice, LORD, lay not this sin to their charge. And
when he had said this, he fell asleep.

II

THE REVELATION OF THE PRIEST OF HUMANITY.

WE have begun by considering, in the first of these Readings, the fact of the Ascension of JESUS CHRIST to the Right Hand of GOD, and the revelation to the human race in that Ascension of man's true home and his abiding state. Further, we have learnt from the Wounds graven on the glorified Body of the Ascended One, that the sufferings of time are the discipline which we must undergo to fit us for eternity,—that we are to go through our life on earth submitting to GOD's Will and yielding to His training, whatever it may cost us, in union with our Ascended LORD.

But the question will arise in our hearts, " Who is sufficient for these things ? " And it must be our business as we proceed to try and find the answer to this question. Recognizing all that is involved in this law of our life, I think we shall see that the vision in the power of which the first martyr was enabled to lay down his life in peace is the vision in which alone the Christian in all ages must live and die : " Lo, I see the Heavens opened, and the Son of Man standing at the Right Hand of GOD ! "

Now if, as has been said, Christian life is a living

union with a living Person, it follows that union with
Him must exist under the conditions, not of His past,
but of His present life; and that, since JESUS CHRIST
has passed into the Heavens, our life on earth must
be one of very real union with our Ascended LORD.
It is difficult for us to realize in any degree what the
Ascended Life of JESUS really is, but we must endeavour
to do so as we meditate on the various presentations
of it given us in GOD's Word.

To-day we will fix our gaze on the vision which
reveals Him to us as our great High Priest ever interceding for us before the Throne of GOD. Again and
again in Holy Scripture this representation of JESUS
as the Living Priest, the Mediator between GOD and
man, is given to us. S. Paul thus writes of Him in
his Epistle to the Romans (chap. viii. ver. 34): "It is
CHRIST that died, yea rather, that is risen again, Who
is even at the Right Hand of GOD, Who also maketh
intercession for us." In the Epistle to the Hebrews
the writer constantly sets Him before us as the Priest
"consecrated for evermore" (Heb. vii. 28.), and for
ever fulfilling that ministry typified by the entrance
year by year into the Most Holy Place of the High
Priest of Israel. Thus we find him saying, a few
verses earlier in the same chapter of that Epistle:
"This Man, because He continueth ever, hath an
unchangeable priesthood. Wherefore He is able to
save them to the uttermost that come unto GOD by
Him, seeing He ever liveth to make intercession for
them." And again in the two following chapters the
same great fact is insisted upon: "We have such an
High Priest, Who is set on the Right Hand of the

Throne of the Majesty in the Heavens; a Minister of the Sanctuary, and of the true Tabernacle, which the LORD pitched and not man " (Heb. viii. 1, 2). "For CHRIST is not entered into the holy places made with hands, which are the figures of the true; but into Heaven itself, now to appear in the Presence of GOD for us " (Heb. ix. 24). In his First General Epistle we find S. John alluding to our LORD's work of priestly intercession when he says: "If any man sin, we have an Advocate with the FATHER, JESUS CHRIST the righteous" (1 S. John ii. 1). And in the Apocalypse we have presented to us the vision of JESUS, at one time as the Priest clad in the priestly garments (Rev. i. 13), and at another as the Victim of His Own Priesthood, the Lamb as it had been slain, pleading for us the merits of His Own Death (Rev. vi. 6).

This is the vision we must gaze on now, and it is the vision of a *present fact.* It is difficult to realize this. We can believe in the marvels of the past, and we are not staggered at the marvels of the future,— but it is hard to grasp the fact that now, in the present, JESUS, as our great High Priest, is continuously acting upon the heart of the Eternal GOD for us,— moment by moment, day by day, night by night,—that at this very moment He is pleading (and so mightily !) for you and for me as He stands before the Throne. Yet so it is; and even now we may look within the Veil and see "JESUS, Who was made a little lower than the Angels, for the suffering of death, crowned with glory and honour," living His Ascended Life in our very humanity, bone of our bone, flesh of our flesh, the Representative of our race, the GOD-conse-

crated Priest, for ever presenting before the FATHER
the consummated Sacrifice of Calvary.   And in this
vision we learn to recognize the fact that we *now*
'' have a great High Priest that is passed into the
Heavens, JESUS the Son of GOD " (Heb. iv. 14).

This truth is very clearly brought out by the old
Law, which is the shadow of good things to come in
the Kingdom of the Resurrection.   In studying the
law of sacrifice as set forth in the Old Tes ament,
we find that what is considered the great crucial act
of sacrifice is not the slaying of the victim, but the
presentation to GOD of the offering already slain,—
that to offer sacrifice never means in the Old Testament the slaying of the offering chosen, but always
implies the bringing of it into the Presence of GOD in
definite oblation.   No victim under the old Law was
ever slain on the Altar.   Some of them were slain at
a distance from it (*e.g.*, Num. xix. 2, 3); some at the
foot of the Altar; but none were slain upon it.   It
was afterwards in every case that the priest brought
the offering which had been slain and laid it upon
the Altar, and when the sacrifice was thus brought
solemnly into the Presence of GOD and presented
before Him, it had power with GOD.   It is in the
ceremonial of the Great Day of Atonement that this
law is brought out most clearly.   (Read Exod. xxx.
10, and Lev. xvi. 11–17.)   On that day the victims
were brought to the door of the Tabernacle and were
there slain ; then the High Priest took of their blood
and sprinkled it first upon the Altar of Incense in
the Holy Place, after which he carried it in conjunc-
tion with incense into the Holy of Holies, and there

sprinkled with it the Mercy Seat itself. It was then that the sacrifice had power with GOD, when the merit of it was pleaded in the Most Holy Place, not at the moment when it was slain. So, when JESUS CHRIST came to be the Priest of Humanity, in order that He might have a victim commensurate in dignity with His own Priesthood, He gave Himself to be slain for the sins of His people,—but then afterwards He passed into the Holy of Holies, into Heaven itself, "now to appear in the Presence of GOD for us" (Heb. ix. 24), there ever to offer before His FATHER the adorable sacrifice of Calvary. This is why the phrase, so often used, which speaks of "the *altar* of the Cross," seems to me to have an unreality about it,—because the Offering *once slain* upon the Cross is continually *offered* in Heaven, as shadowed forth in the death and presentation of the victims under the Jewish Law. And what is the effect of this Offering? As our great High Priest presents His sacrifice to the FATHER, He is continually claiming from the FATHER all the pledged fruits of His obedient life and redeeming death. That which He merited for us on earth, that He now claims for us in Heaven; the Eternal Son, as He now presents before the FATHER the death He once died on Calvary, is claiming for you and for me all those graces in the strength of which we can rise up from the far country of sin and enter into our Father's House.

This is what JESUS CHRIST is doing now,—not repeating His Sacrifice,—GOD forbid! "We are sanctified through the offering of the Body of JESUS CHRIST once for all!" (Heb. x. 10). The Sacrifice *has* been

offered, the salvation *is* won, the death can never be
repeated; but that One mighty Death is being at this
moment and every moment pleaded continuously before the Throne of GOD, and upon that continuous
presentation to GOD depends the efficacy of the Sacrifice for the salvation and sanctification of our souls.
There is one theological truth which brings this out
very forcibly, and it is this: It has always been held
by theologians that beyond the Day of Judgment
there can be no further victories of the Precious Blood,
because the perpetual pleading of the Sacrifice offered
on Calvary will then have ceased, and therefore man's
state will then be fixed.   True it is that it has come
to be the popular belief amongst us that man's state
is fixed at death, but that is because the true conception of the Intermediate State has been allowed to
drop out of our modern theology.   As a fact, we know
no limits to the possibilities of grace in the Intermediate
State; not at death, but after judgment, according to
the vision granted to S. John, come the awful words:
"He that is unjust, let him be unjust still; and he
which is filthy, let him be filthy still; and he that is
righteous, let him be righteous still; and he that is
holy, let him be holy still!" (Rev. xxii. 11; see chap.
xx. 11–13).   Why is this?   For this reason: Before our
LORD takes His place on the Judgment Seat to execute that final judicial function which, in the supreme
justice of GOD, is committed to Him, "because He is
the Son of Man," (S. John v. 22, 27; see Acts xvii. 31)
He will have ceased to exercise His office as Intercessor.   We know that His mediatorial action is a
transitory one, belonging to the present condition of

things in the Kingdom of GOD ; and until that is over
His intercession is of prevailing power with GOD for
His people, here and in Paradise. But when He
ceases to intercede, then fixity of state for man will
be reached, for the Atonement made on Calvary will
no longer be operative for the souls on behalf of whom
JESUS will have ceased to plead. This truth brings
home to us the fact, that our only hope of attaining
finally the true end of our being,—a hope reaching
through our life both here and in the Intermediate
State, —lies in the perpetual pleading in the Presence
of the FATHER by the Eternal Son of the death He
once died upon the Cross.

As the outcome of this subject there are certain
simple thoughts which it behoves us now to gather up.

And first, we learn that the intercession of JESUS
CHRIST before the Throne in Heaven is all-embracing.
Wide as are the limits within which the fruits of His
Passion are efficacious, so wide are the limits of the
action of His intercession ; as He died for all once
on Calvary, so He pleads for all now in Heaven.
Secondly, we have to realize that, as His intercession
is thus all-embracing, so is it also individual and par-
ticular. Just as it is true that on Calvary He died
for each as well as for all,—as there He suffered con-
sciously for each individual soul, so that you and I
may look up to Him and say, "The Son of GOD
loved *me*, and gave Himself for *me*" (Gal. ii. 20), so
is it true that all through my life here, and through
every moment of it in the Intermediate State, He is
and will be pleading for me. For not only is the
intercession of JESUS CHRIST universal in its embrace,

but it is also individual. And thirdly, in His intercession there meet these three things: (*A.*) Perfect
knowledge of individual needs. "He knoweth the
way that I take" (Job xxiii. 10). He measures accu-
rately the forces that tempt me ; He measures accu-
rately my strength to resist the temptation. Better
than I know them myself my needs are known to
Him, and He is always claiming for me moment by
moment that which He sees to be needful to enable
me in the living present to persevere in the strife, and
to win the victory over self and sin. (*B.*) Fulness of
sympathy. "We have not an High Priest that cannot
be touched with the feeling of our infirmities, but was
in all points tempted like as we are, yet without sin"
(Heb. iv. 15). Therefore He pleads for me with the
fullest yearning of His tender, sympathizing Heart,
since it is not only from without that He knows my
trials, but He knows them from a like experience.
It matters not what the trouble is,—

> " In every pang that rends the heart
> The Man of Sorrows had a part ;
> He sympathizes with our grief,
> And to the sufferer sends relief."

Is it pain that wears away thy bodily strength ? Who
ever suffered as He did. Listen to the prophetic
revelation of those sufferings, no word of which passed
His lips as He endured them : " I am poured out
like water, all My bones are out of joint, My heart
also in the midst of My body is even like melting
wax ; I am dried up like a potsherd, and My tongue
cleaveth to my gums, and Thou hast brought Me into

the dust of death.   They pierced My hands and My
feet; I may tell all My bones" (Ps. xxii. 14–17).
Is it sorrow that wrings thy heart?   Did not He shed
tears at the grave of His friend?   Did He not know
the pang of disappointment when all His disciples for-
sook Him and fled?   the anguish of separation when
He hung upon the Cross and His Mother stood by?
Is it the loneliness of want of sympathy, of not being
understood, which wounds and jars upon thee?   How
awful was the isolation of Jesus!   How pathetically
suggestive is the Gospel story when it tells of His
craving for human sympathy, and of the quiet patience
with which He put that craving aside when again and
again even His disciples failed to understand Him!
(See S. Luke xviii. 31–34, and ii. 48–50; S. John
xii. 16.)   Is it the exhaustion of fierce temptation,
the agony of soul-darkness, that weighs thee down?
Was He not "in all points" tempted in the wilderness?   Did He not cry with an exceeding great and
bitter cry out of the anguish of His soul, " Eloi,
Eloi, lama sabachthani?"   Believe me, it matters
not what the grief is which presses so heavily upon
thee; our great High Priest, JESUS the Son of GOD, has
known the agony of a like experience.   (C.) And in
His intercession there is not only fulness of knowledge of thy needs, and fulness of sympathy with them,
but there is also fulness of confidence in pleading for
the satisfaction of them.   "I will pray the FATHER,
and He shall give you another Comforter, that He
may abide with you for ever, even the Spirit of Truth "
(S. John xiv. 16, 17).   For as He stands before the
Throne of GOD pleading the sacrifice of His death, He

knows that He is simply claiming for His people the pledged fruits of His Passion ; and thus, in the fulness of knowledge, of sympathy, and of confidence, JESUS CHRIST is interceding ceaselessly for you and for me. Do we need guidance, peace of conscience, strength in weakness, consolation in distress, protection in danger? He claims them for us; He is claiming them now. Oh, if we could but lay hold with lively faith on this simple fact, we should go on our way realizing in deepest conviction, what is indeed true,— that no one knows what it is to live until he has learnt to live his life in union with the Ascended JESUS !

Lastly, let us recognise the law of spiritual life which is revealed to us in the light that streams from this vision of our great High Priest that is passed into the Heavens. Heaven seems to us (is it not true ?) so far away, a "land that is very far off,"—the thought of the Intercessor standing before the Throne of GOD in Heaven is to us so difficult to grasp,—how shall the great truth of His present and continual intercession for us be brought home to our very senses, within the limits of our very life? Behold the Mystery of the Altar ! There in solemn reality He stoops to uplift before the Throne of GOD, in union with His perpetual intercession in Heaven, the oblation of Bread and Wine which He instituted and has commanded us to con- tinue as a perpetual memory of His Death and Passion; and in the mystery of that great Sacrament on earth the mystery of His Ministry in Heaven becomes to us an intelligible fact. Ceaseless as is the presentation of His death in Heaven, so ceaseless is its presentation on earth. For in the universal worship of Christendom the prophecy of Malachi is fulfilled : "From the rising of the sun unto the going down of the same My Name shall be great among the Gentiles, and in every place incense shall be offered unto My Name, and a pure offering, for My Name shall be great among the heathen, saith the LORD of Hosts" (Mal. i. 11). 'Tis always morning somewhere, and through the ministry of the daily Sacrifice the presentation of CHRIST's death on Calvary is ceaseless on earth as it is in Heaven.

Beneath the shadow of GOD's Altar live, then, thy life ; beyond it let thy gaze of faith penetrate to see Heaven opened and JESUS standing at the Right Hand of GOD, pleading for thee His Passion in the Most Holy Place. Know that, through the ceaseless presentation of that One All-sufficient Sacrifice there, the Precious Blood is ever crying to the FATHER in Heaven,—know that, through the ceaseless presentation of the "perpetual memory" of that Sacrifice here, the Precious Blood is ever crying to the FATHER on earth. And realizing this truth, thou shalt live thy life trusting for the supply of all thy needs, and of the needs of those near and dear to thee, to the continual pleading of that great Sacrifice in the Presence of GOD by Him Who is the crowned High Priest of Humanity.

> " Be still, my soul, for GOD is near,
>   The great High Priest is with thee now ;
> The LORD of Life Himself is here,
>   Before Whose Face the Angels bow.

.   .   .   .   .   .

" He pleads before the Mercy Seat,
　　He pleads with GOD, He pleads for thee,
　He gives thee Bread from Heaven to eat,
　　His Flesh and Blood in mystery.

" I come, O LORD, for Thou dost call,
　　To blend my pleading prayer with Thine ;
　To Thee I give myself, my all,
　　And feed on Thee and make Thee mine."

Third Reading.

EPHESIANS vi. 7-10.

BUT unto every one of us is given grace according to the
measure of the gift of CHRIST. Wherefore he saith,
When He ascended up on high, He led captivity captive, and gave gifts unto men. Now that He ascended,
what is it but that He also descended first into the lower
parts of the earth? He that descended is the same also
that ascended up far above all heavens, that He might
fill all things.

c

III.

THE REVELATION OF THE KING OF HUMANITY.

WE have already recognized the fact that it is with great difficulty we can realize what the Ascended Life of JESUS CHRIST is, and is *to us*, in such a way as to make it bear with living power on our own daily life. And we have sought to meet this difficulty by considering the Ascension of JESUS CHRIST, first as the . revelation to man of his true and abiding state, and of the conditions under which alone that state can be attained,—and secondly, as the procession from earth to Heaven of the High Priest of Humanity, there to present in the true Holy of Holies the consummated sacrifice of His Death on Calvary.

We have now to dwell on another aspect of His Ascended Life, and to see in the day on which we commemorate His Ascension the Festival of the Coronation of JESUS CHRIST ; since it was at His Ascension that our LORD was throned at the Right Hand of GOD, and crowned with the crown of pure gold which the FATHER hath set upon His Head; so that henceforth the Church greets Him with the enraptured cry, "Thou art the King of Glory, O CHRIST !" Once more let us turn to the Word of God, and in the Epistle to the

Hebrews read what is said of the Regal, as before we read of the Priestly, Office of our LORD. Pursuing his system of drawing out the meaning of the Old Scriptures as interpreting and interpreted by the New, the writer quotes from the Eighth Psalm, and comments upon the words he quotes, thus: "One in a certain place testified, saying, *What is man, that Thou art mindful of him? or the son of man, that Thou visitest him? Thou madest him a little lower than the angels, Thou crownedst him with glory and honour, and didst set him over the works of Thy Hands; Thou hast put all things in subjection under his feet.* For in that He put all in subjection under Him, He left nothing that is not put under Him. But now we see not yet all things put under Him. But we see JESUS, Who was made a little lower than the angels, for the suffering of death, crowned with glory and honour" (Heb. ii. 6–9). And farther on he adds: "Wherefore . . . let us run with patience the race that is set before us, looking unto JESUS, the Author and Finisher of our faith, Who, for the joy that was set before Him, endured the Cross, despising the shame, and is set down at the Right Hand of the Throne of GOD" (Heb. xii. 1, 2). S. Peter seems to bear ever in mind the Kingly Office of our Ascended LORD, as is shown by brief allusions both in his sermons and epistles, such as his words in the fifth chapter of the Acts of the Apostles: "Him hath GOD exalted with His Right Hand to be a Prince and a Saviour" (Acts v. 31); and in his First Epistle: "JESUS CHRIST, Who is gone into Heaven, and is on the Right Hand of GOD; angels and authorities and powers being made subject unto Him"

(1 Peter iii. 21, 22). And in the Book of the Revelation we find the vision of Him not only as "the Lamb slain from the foundation of the world," but also as the Mighty One Who "hath on His vesture and on His thigh a name written, KING OF KINGS, and LORD OF LORDS" (Rev. xix. 16).

We are, then, now to consider our Ascended LORD as the bountiful King, distributing to mankind as His subjects His manifold gifts of grace. But, before going further we must have clearly before our minds three things: First, that before our LORD, as the Ascended King of all the earth, could give His gifts to mankind, He had to merit them in His sinless Humanity on earth. All the gifts needed by us for our salvation and perfection, He merited by His obedient life crowned by His obedient death; so that, when JESUS CHRIST brought His life on earth to a close, by bowing His Head on Calvary and resigning His Spirit into His Father's Hands, He had merited for us all we need. All that is needed by each one of us for our cleansing from the stains of a guilty past; all that is needed by each one of us for the liberating of our sin-bound souls in the living present; all that is needed by each one of us for the perfecting of our imperfect characters in the unknown future,—all was perfectly merited for each, for all, of the sons of men, when JESUS CHRIST crowned the obedience of His life by the obedience of His death.

Secondly, having thus merited the gifts which can satisfy all our needs, yet ere He can bestow those gifts on His people He must claim them for His own. And so JESUS CHRIST stands before mankind not only as the

High Priest continually presenting before the FATHER
His all-suffering merits, but also as the victorious
King continuously receiving from the FATHER the
gifts He has merited and now claims for His own
possession.   He reigns as King because He pleads
as Priest.   This brings us back to the remarkable
passage in S. Paul's Epistle to the Ephesians which
stands at the commencement of this Reading.   You
will have noticed the very striking alteration made
by the Apostle in his quotation from the Sixty-eighth
Psalm.   The two passages are not contradictory but
complementary one of the other; the Psalmist points
to our Ascended LORD as the enthroned King Who
in His assumed Humanity is receiving gifts from
GOD: "Thou hast ascended on high; Thou hast
led captivity captive; Thou hast received gifts for
men (or, as the margin gives it, *in the Man*), yea
for the rebellious also, that the LORD GOD might
dwell among them;" while S. Paul points out that
He receives in order that He may give, and shows
us what the gifts are which, as the bountiful King,
He is distributing to His people, and why it is His to
give them : "Unto every one is given grace according
to the measure of the gift of CHRIST.   Wherefore he
saith, *When He ascended up on high, He led captivity
captive, and gave gifts unto men.*   Now that He
ascended, what is it but that He also descended first
into the lower parts of the earth?   He that descended
is the same also that ascended up far above all
Heavens, that He might fill all things " (Ephes. iv.
7-10).   For this Kingship of JESUS which we are
now considering is not the divine power which as

God is His from all eternity, but the delegated power which He has received from the FATHER as the Representative of Humanity. The gifts vouchsafed to us are the gifts of GoD, but they come to us through the One King of Humanity, the Man CHRIST JESUS.

Thirdly, if we turn to the Old Testament we shall see how markedly this enthronement of the Crucified One was foreseen again and again by the prophets of Israel in the revelations vouchsafed to them. For example, let us take the well-known prophecies of Zechariah; there we read : " I will pour upon the house of David, and upon the inhabitants of Jerusalem, the spirit of grace and of supplications, and they shall look upon Me Whom they have pierced, and they shall mourn for Him as one mourneth for his only son, and shall be in bitterness for Him as one that is in bitterness for his first-born " (Zech. xii. 10). What is the vision presented to us here? We see Him that was despised and rejected of men now raised by GOD to His Right Hand, and set on His Throne as King of Zion, and thence pouring on a rebellious race the grace of conversion. And when this prophecy was fulfilled by the conversion of the Jews after Pentecost, S. Peter declared it to be the gift of Him Whom "ye have taken, and by wicked hands have crucified and slain. This JESUS hath GOD raised up, whereof we all are witnesses. Therefore, being by the Right Hand of GOD exalted, and having received of the FATHER the promise of the HOLY GHOST, He hath shed forth this which ye now see and hear" (Acts ii. 23, 32, 33). Thus we get before our minds the vision which we have now to contemplate,—the vision of JESUS our

Elder Brother, the Representative of Humanity, revealed to us as possessing of right, as the result of
His Passion and Intercession, the gifts of GOD in all
their fulness; and distributing those gifts to man in
the free exercise of His Kingly power, yet in accordance with the Will of GOD, and in the measure corre-
sponding to the degree of each man's receptivity.

Every kind of grace we need for our sanctification
comes, then, to us from the Ascended JESUS. (*A.*)
It is JESUS Who brings men to Himself in the power
of Prevenient Grace. The meaning of "prevenient"
is this: that none will seek the LORD until the LORD
seeks them; and so every drawing of the soul to GOD
of which every one is conscious from time to time,
even while living in a state of sin, all awakenings of
memory, all arisings of holy aspiration, are due solely
to prevenient grace; for JESUS goes out seeking
the salvation of the lost; and not only through the
agencies of the Church, but also beyond the limits of
the Church, He is thus ever, in His mercy, seeking
souls. That this prevenient grace is the gift of the
Ascended JESUS, is revealed to us in that which is
considered as the typical conversion. The story of
the conversion of S. Paul is told to us as a pattern of
the way in which souls are brought back to GOD; and
we know when and how there came to him the grace
which convinced his intellect and bowed his will,—he
was met by the Ascended JESUS as he was on the road
to Damascus. The voice which spoke to him was the
voice of the Ascended One; the power which mas-
tered him was the power of the Ascended One; and
thus we learn that it is JESUS Who gives prevenient

grace. (*B.*) Again, it is the Ascended JESUS Who
gives Absolving Grace. He alone has the power of
absolution, as He says Himself: "The Son of Man
hath power on earth to forgive sins" (S. Mark ii. 10),
i.e., the delegated power committed to Him by GOD.
Now, there is a school of teachers who, in their en-
deavours to attract souls to GOD, deal with them in
this way: they lead them to conviction of sin; they
point to Calvary; they tell them that JESUS on the
Cross merited forgiveness for all; they bid them believe and claim that forgiveness, and go on their way
rejoicing. That is, they teach that all men are forgiven, and that all they have to do is to believe that
they are forgiven,—that absolution is no real communication of pardon, that baptism is no real change of
state. But what is the truth? We have learned that
our LORD, having died for all upon the Cross, ever
stands at the Right Hand of GOD pleading for each,
moment by moment, that One Death. Further,
that having by His Death merited forgiveness for
all, He ever claims for each, moment by moment,
that forgiveness. But then, having merited forgiveness and claimed forgiveness for all, He is ever
able and willing to speak forgiveness to each. And
if you and I are to benefit by the free pardon
which He has won for us, it is as necessary that
He speak that pardon individually to each soul as
that He merit it for all. "If we confess our sins,
He is faithful and just to forgive us our sins, and to
cleanse us from all unrighteousness" (1 John i. 9).
JESUS has power on earth to forgive sins by the absolving power delegated to Him, and as by prevenient

grace He brings men back to Himself, so by absolving grace He cleanses men from the guilt of past sins. (*C.*) Further, it is the Ascended LORD Who gives Justifying Grace. Having sought out the wandering soul in the far country of sin, having loosed it from the burden of a guilty past, He carries on increasingly the work of its justification in the present. He reveals to us as we can bear it our sins and their sinfulness; He leads us on to brave grappling with temptation; He pours His healing grace into the wounds of our souls; He upholds our stumbling feet, so that we learn to sing, "Though I fall, I shall not be cast away, for the LORD upholdeth me with His Hand,"—He sets us free from the tyranny of self and sin in the present. It is JESUS Who gives justifying grace. (*D.*) And it is the Ascended LORD Who gives Sanctifying Grace. He sheds the light of His truth upon the intellect and His love into the heart; He enables the will so that the hands that hang down are lifted up and the feeble knees become strong and do great things. He it is Who clothes with power them that minister for Him, Who gives them the word they should speak, and the energy and reality that ring out in their tones as they speak it,— He it is Who can make of unlearned Apostles champions meet to contend with the keenest intellects of earth,—He it is Who gives to each of His people the gifts of grace needed for the perfecting of the character. And not only to those on earth does JESUS give these gifts of grace, but to those also who have passed into Paradise. The light in which they rejoice, the love which beats in their heart, the power in which they

triumph in their wondrous liberty, is communicated
to them moment by moment by the Royal bounty of
their Ascended King. On earth and in Paradise "the
eyes of all wait upon Thee, O LORD, and Thou givest
them their meat in due season." It is JESUS Who
gives sanctifying grace.

There is one thing more for us to notice here, and
that is by what agency He, the enthroned King, gives
to His people the gifts they need. It is by sending
to them the gift of gifts, the gift of the HOLY GHOST.
JESUS CHRIST won for us the supply of all our needs,
because He merited for us by His Passion and claims
for us by His ceaseless Intercession the one great
gift in which all others meet, the characteristic gift of
the Christian Life, the gift of the indwelling HOLY
SPIRIT. The HOLY GHOST was working on men from
without all through the ages before our LORD came ;
He was in Jewry, as He is (who can doubt it?) in
heathendom ; but, said our LORD, " The Spirit of
Truth dwelleth with you and shall be *in* you " (S. John
xiv. 17); and having merited for us this gift, the
Ascended LORD now claims as the fruit of His Passion the right to send to us the HOLY GHOST to dwell
in us, and to communicate to us all the manifold gifts
of grace. " Know ye not that ye are the temple of GOD,
and that the Spirit of GOD dwelleth in you ? " (1 Cor.
iii. 16). It is by the guidance of the HOLY SPIRIT that
JESUS leads us back from the far country of sin to our
FATHER'S Home ; it is by the action of the indwelling
Spirit that JESUS brings us into union with Himself ;
for when we yield ourselves up as loyal subjects to the
power of our Ascended King, JESUS makes us, through

the action of the HOLY SPIRIT, bone of His bone and flesh of His flesh, very members incorporate of His mystical Body. As the sap flows from the trunk of the tree into every one of its branches, so the supply of grace stored in the Ascended Life of JESUS flows from Him into us His members through the continuous action of the Spirit of GOD.

Thus, then, JESUS stands revealed to us as the Enthróned King, giving all gifts unto men by giving to them His special gift, the indwelling Spirit of GOD. By His Spirit He cleanses us; by His Spirit He enables us; by His Spirit He communicates to us "of His fulness,"—and Christian Life is this: to be ever living under the eye of our King in the Heavenly Palace, and ever fed by His bountiful Hand. But to do this we need the grace of receptivity; that is, the power to take from the Hand of JESUS all the gifts and all the graces He desires to give us; and for this let us make our prayer unto Him, that the withered hands of our wavering faith may be stretched forth to receive and strengthened to hold all that He waits to give.

Let this, then, be my endeavour to-day : kneeling at His Feet—(for Heaven is His throne, but earth is His footstool, where, if I seek Him, I shall surely find Him !)—to look up into His Face and see the eye of thé Ascended One fixed on me in love; and then to give myself up, in humblest worship and whole-hearted self-oblation, to Him Who is the Enthroned King of Humanity, and Who Himself, of His Royal bounty, will supply all my need.

Fourth Reading.

EPHESIANS i. 20-23.

GOD hath raised Him from the dead, and set Him at His Own Right Hand in the Heavenly Places, far above all principality, and power, and might, and dominion, and every name that is named, not only in this world, but also in that which is to come; and hath put all things under His Feet, and gave Him to be the Head over all things to the Church, which is His Body, the Fulness of Him that filleth all in all.

IV.

THE REVELATION OF THE ORGANISM OF THE CHURCH.

In the revelations of our Ascended Lord which we have already considered we have learnt to recognize this great truth, that the gifts of God come to man through the power He has delegated to the Priest and King of Humanity; and thus we find ourselves face to face with the mediatorial work of Jesus Christ in Heaven, and we learn that it is a work of priestly intercession before God, and of kingly munificence towards man. "There is One Mediator between God and man, the Man Christ Jesus" (1 Tim. ii. 5).

To-day we have to dwell on another revelation given us by the Holy Ghost in the Word of God, and it is that which is set before us in that great theological utterance of S. Paul in his Epistle to the Ephesians which stands at the commencement of this Reading : "God hath set Him at His Own Right Hand in the Heavenly Places, . . . and hath put all things under His Feet, and gave Him to be the Head over all things to the Church, which is His Body, the Fulness of Him that filleth all in all" (Eph. i. 20, 22, 23). The vision presented to us here is that of our Ascended Lord as the Head of a great spiritual society which S. Paul calls "the Church, which is His Body." And the subject which we have therefore to consider is that mysterious union between CHRIST and His Church on which the Apostle here, as in other passages of his writings, so strongly insists.

And here I must say a word of explanation as to the necessity (from which, in speaking of the Church of JESUS CHRIST, I cannot escape) of traversing again some of the ground covered in our meditations on the Risen Life of our LORD. So deep is this great truth of the relation of the Church to its LORD, so difficult is it to apprehend, that, it is only when it is brought before us again and again, and our minds learn to ponder it as did the Saints of old under the guidance of the HOLY SPIRIT, that we slowly get a grasp of its true meaning. And therefore, as I believe, some measure of repetition in considering this subject may not be altogether without profit.

Now, as a matter of fact, the Catholic Church exists at this moment, and has existed for more than eighteen centuries. It consists of the great company of the Baptized as they live banded together in a society which possesses certain distinct marks whereby it may be recognized. Notice, it does *not* consist simply of the great multitude of all baptized souls as a mass of unorganized material; it consists of the great company of the baptized living their life as GOD wills them to live it, banded together in the unity of that society which was founded by JESUS CHRIST Himself, and which possesses certain distinguishing notes or features. If we turn to Holy Scripture, we find these mentioned in a picture of the Church in very early

days which is sketched for us in the Acts of the
Apostles: "Then they that gladly received his word
were baptized, and the same day there were added
unto them about three thousand souls. And they
continued stedfastly in the Apostles' doctrine and
fellowship, and in breaking of bread, and in prayers"
(Acts ii. 41, 42). We find in these words three distinct features of the Church of CHRIST: every society
of Christians that possesses these features is a part of
the Catholic Church; and no society that lacks these
features, though it may be a gathering of Christian
men, is a part of that Historic Society founded on
earth by JESUS CHRIST.

I. "They continued in the Apostles' Fellowship."
It is by the perpetuation of an Authorized Ministry
that the great principle of Continuity is maintained in
the Church. When our LORD bade His disciples go
into all the world and preach the Gospel, His words
were: "Lo, I am with you alway, even unto the end
of the world,"—and from them we learn that His
Church is to exist as a visible historic society till
JESUS comes again. And it is for the maintenance
of this continuity of the Church that the Apostolic
Ministry was constituted. During the forty days our
LORD remained on earth after He had called His
Church into being on the first Easter Day, He met
"the Apostles whom He had chosen," and spoke to
them "of the things pertaining to the Kingdom of
GOD" (Acts i. 2, 3). He said to them, "All power
is given unto Me in Heaven and in earth,"—here is
the claim to kingly authority; then comes the delega-
tion of that authority: "Go ye therefore and teach all
D

nations, baptizing them in the Name of the FATHER,
and of the SON, and of the HOLY GHOST;" and then
He goes on: "Teaching them" (those thus gathered
into the fold) "to observe all things whatsoever I have
commanded you;" and then there is the final promise
of personal direction and control: "Lo, I am with
you alway, even unto the consummation of the ages"
(S. Matt. xxviii. 18–20). Here is the GOD-given com-
mission, within the GOD-created Church, of the Apos-
tolate; and accordingly, when on the Day of Pentecost
the first great in-gathering took place, and there were
added unto the Church of CHRIST about three thousand souls, we read that "they continued stedfastly
in the Apostles' fellowship," learning the truth from
their lips and yielding obedience to their directions.
This GOD-appointed Ministry constitutes, according
to the graphic imagery of S. Paul, the "joints and
bands," the outer framework, of the mystic body of
CHRIST, holding it in union with its Head, the means
whereby nourishment is ministered to it from Him,
that it may be increased with the increase of GOD
(Col. ii. 19). And in that passage of the Epistle to
the Ephesians which we considered yesterday, in
which S. Paul tells us that when our LORD ascended
into Heaven He gave gifts unto men, he goes on to
tell us further what some of these gifts were: "And
He gave some apostles, and some prophets, and some
evangelists, and some pastors and teachers; for the
perfecting of the saints, for the work of the ministry,
for the edifying of the body of CHRIST;" and then
he explains what is the object with which these gifts
are bestowed: "That we . . . may grow up into

Him in all things which is the Head, even CHRIST,
from whom the whole body, fitly joined together, and
compacted by that which every joint supplieth, according to the effectual working in the measure of
every part, maketh increase of the body unto the
edifying of itself in love" (Eph. iv. 11, 12, 15, 16).
The living Ministry, then, is the external framework
of the Church ; by its continuity the continuity of the
Church is maintained ; and thus we see that through
the Apostolic Ministry commissioned by JESUS CHRIST
before His Ascension, and perpetuated ever since, the
Apostolic Society founded by JESUS CHRIST before
His Ascension lives on as an abiding fact throughout
the ages.   Every society of Christians, therefore, that
possesses the threefold or Apostolic Ministry possesses
the first note of the Catholic Church of CHRIST.

II. "They continued in the Apostles' Doctrine."
The second feature of the Christian Church is the
Apostolic Doctrine.   There may be a society possessing the threefold ministry in unbroken succession, and
yet that society may not be a living branch of the
Catholic Church, through having lost its hold on the
true faith and fallen into heresy.   For the disciples
continued not only in the Apostles' fellowship, but
also in the Apostles' doctrine ; and where any part of
the Church has fallen into heresy, its channel is dry
and the living waters of truth and grace do not flow.
So, then, every branch of the Church must teach as
the truth of GOD all that is dogmatically declared to
be GOD's truth in the three creeds formulated in the
first ages by the undivided Church of CHRIST; and
also any truth which, although not embodied in the

creeds, has yet always been received as the truth of
GOD throughout the limits of the Christian Church.
Any branch of the Church that would deny the truth
of any one of the three creeds would be guilty of dis-
loyalty to the Head of the Church; any branch of
the Church that would deny the efficacy of Prayer or
the authority of the Word of GOD would fall into the
same error. For, though the *nature* of the inspiration
of Holy Scripture has never been defined, the *reality*
of its inspiration has never been denied all through
the ages in the Christian Church; and, similarly,
everywhere and always throughout the Church, the efficacy of Prayer, while never explained, has never been
challenged. But notice, the realm of dogma is very
definite, but its extent is not very wide; and we must
be careful not to raise to the authoritative level of
dogmatic utterance what are really only pious beliefs
not to be enforced on other minds. The Church of
CHRIST remained undivided until, in the providence of
GOD, the two great dogmas or doctrines of the Holy
Trinity, Three Persons in One GOD, and of the Incarnation of our LORD JESUS CHRIST, had been declared
and safe-guarded,—and then the dogmatic age of the
Church passed away. Thenceforward she has never
been able to give authoritative expression to any dogmatic utterance; nor has there been any need, because
in those two great truths is summed up the whole
Christian Revelation. Thus we see that every branch
of the Church which teaches as authoritative truth the
three creeds and those other doctrines which have
never been questioned throughout the Church, possesses (in spite of controversies on a number of other

points which may seem to us like dogma because
they are so dear to us personally), possesses, I say,
another note of the Catholic Church of CHRIST.

'III. "They continued in Breaking of Bread and in
Prayers." The third note of the Christian Church is
the maintenance throughout her limits of the two
great Sacraments ordained by CHRIST Himself, and
of United Worship. Wherever the ministry of Baptism
and of the Holy Eucharist is lacking, wherever the
assembling together for Public Worship is lacking,
there we miss one essential feature of the Christian
Church. But wherever, in any society of Christians,
we find the Sacraments of Baptism and of the LORD's
Supper given their due position in the Christian
scheme, wherever people gather together age after age
in GOD's House to carry on the worship of GOD in
GOD's way, there we find another note of the Catholic
Church. And it is an undeniable fact that in almost
every land you come across this Society, calling itself
the Church of CHRIST, claiming to be continued by
the Apostolic Ministry, to teach the Apostolic Doctrine, and to maintain the Christian Worship in all its
features as expressed in the liturgies handed down
from the earliest times in the Christian Church. True
it is that this essential unity is not universally expressed
in external union ; but as truly as the natural Body of
JESUS CHRIST, when it hung upon the Cross, though
every bone was out of joint, was yet the Body of the
Incarnate GOD, so truly is the Society created by
Him, though disjointed by many external differences,
the mystical Body of the Incarnate GOD on earth,—
for it is knit together by community of (1) Apostolic

Ministry, (2) Apostolic Doctrine, and (3) Apostolic
Worship, in obedience to His command.

This Church, then, which is "the Body of CHRIST,"
exists on earth to-day, but it exists not only on earth.
We can conceive of it as existing only on earth on
the day of its foundation; though even then we may
. surely believe that those faithful souls who had been
made ready through ages of expectation before the
Coming of the LORD had already their place within
its limits.   But soon one member of the Church of
CHRIST, and then another, would pass into the ranks
of the Departed in Paradise, yet would not therefore
cease to be in the Church, for union with the Church
depends on union with the Head of the Church, and
that union lives on through time and through eternity.   Not only on earth, then, but in Paradise we
see the Church gradually becoming a great fact.   One
by one the Master has been calling thither those made
ready for that day, and as they pass out of our sight
we learn to realize that there, in Paradise, as on earth,
are gathering the members of the mystical Society,
"waiting for the adoption, to wit, the redemption of
our body" (Rom. viii. 23).   But little is told us in
the Word of GOD about the present state of those
blessed ones who have entered into rest.   "The souls
of the faithful are in the Hand of GOD" (Wisdom
iii. 1), and there we leave them with fullest confidence.
Yet some lights are given us even here.   We learn
that the life of the Church in Paradise as on earth is
an organized life; we see in vision the Four Living
Creatures, the Twenty-four Elders, the One hundred
and forty-four thousand Chosen Ones that follow the

Lamb whithersoever He goeth, the Great Multitude
that no man can number, gathered before the Throne
of GOD.   What it means we know not, what the organ-
ization is we cannot explain, but that the principle of
order and of subordination lives on in the Church in
Paradise is clear.

Further, the Church of JESUS CHRIST not only
exists on earth and in Paradise, but its Head is in
Heaven ; and this vast company,—the Ascended LORD
in Heaven, His people resting in Paradise, His people
struggling on earth,—make up one Being.   " The
Church is His Body, the Fulness of Him that filleth
all in all."   The CHRIST never exists before GOD as
an isolated individual, but always as made up of the
Head and the members, CHRIST in union with His
Church.   This truth is one which it is most difficult
to grasp ; bear with me, therefore, if I repeat it once
more.   The Church on earth and in Paradise form
with CHRIST in Heaven one organism,—living in the
union of incorporation with the very Manhood of the
Ascended LORD,—for " we are members of His Body,
of His flesh, and of His bones."   Never should we
regard the Church as independent of CHRIST, as
merely a tool created for Him to use ; the Church is
one with CHRIST by the union of incorporation, and
to think of the Church as a Society founded indeed
by CHRIST, but having a being independent of Him, is
to have a false conception of the Church.   The vision
which GOD has given us in the Scriptures is of CHRIST
as the Head of the Body, of the Church as the mystical Body of CHRIST.

We have then to face the question,—Why has

CHRIST called the Church into existence? And we must begin our answer to this question by asking another,—What is the relation of the Church to CHRIST?

Now notice, the Church is said to be His Body; it is never said to be His Mind, or His Heart, or His Will, or even His Human Spirit, but His Body. And what the relation of the body is to the head, *naturally*, that the relation of the Church to CHRIST in Heaven is *spiritually*. Now, what is the relation of the natural body to the head? Is not the body the instrument which carries out the inspirations of the head? Every movement of my body is dictated by my brain. Whither my brain bids me go, thither I go; what my brain bids me do, that I do; what my brain bids me speak, that I say. Every action of my body, even such as is mechanical,—as, for instance, breathing,—takes place in obedience to the dictates of the head. And precisely the same is true with regard to our LORD JESUS CHRIST. Perhaps this will be more clear to us if we recall the fact that there are three aspects under which the Body of our LORD is presented to our thought. First, there is the human Body which He took of Mary at His Incarnation, when He became " Man of the substance of His mother, born in the world;" secondly, there is His mystical Body which S. Paul tells us is the Church; and thirdly, there is His Sacramental Body by which He nourishes our spiritual life. Now, what is the relation of the human Body of JESUS to the Divine Personality to Which it is united? The Eternal Son comes from Heaven to earth; He assumes our nature for this purpose, that through the words

He speaks and the deeds He does by means of His
human Body He may reveal GOD to man. Through
the human lips of JESUS the revelation of GOD's Truth
reaches our minds ; through the human hands of JESUS
the gifts of GOD's Love reach our hearts. In the days
of His life on earth they who would receive the truth
of GOD received it by drawing nigh to JESUS and
"hearkening to the voice of His words,"—they who
would receive the grace of GOD received it by drawing
nigh to JESUS and seeking contact with His humanity,
—as S. John puts it : "Grace and truth came by
JESUS CHRIST" (S. John i. 17). This, then, is an
abiding law of the Kingdom of GOD,—:hat His gifts
flow to us through the sacred humanity of JESUS
CHRIST. But the time comes when JESUS passes into
Heaven ; how are we on earth to have contact with
His humanity now ? Is it merely by the contemplation of the intellect as it struggles after truth ? by the
longing of the affections as they soar in desire ? Nay ;
if we are to receive of the virtue that goes out of Him
there must be real contact with His humanity still,—
but how ? Just as, in creating His human Body,
CHRIST wedded to His Eternal Person the dust of the
earth, so, in creating His mystical Body, He weds to
Himself the poor sons and daughters of humanity ;
He stretches forth His Hands to draw them unto
Himself, that, incorporated into His mystical Society,
they may become "members of His Body, of His
flesh, and of His bones." This Society, this mystical
Body of CHRIST, is the organism whereby, even while
He is in Heaven, He is still present on earth and still
acts on earth. The Church is not the delegated re-

presentative of an *absent* CHRIST; it is the living organism whereby the *present* CHRIST still acts on earth.
By the feet of the Church's members the sacred Feet
of JESUS still tread the earth; by the voice of the
Church's members His sacred Lips still teach divine
truth; by the hands of the Church's members His
sacred Hands still minister healing to the sores of
humanity. "Go *ye*," are His words, and minister to
all nations the word of truth, the gifts of grace,—for,
"lo! *I* am with you alway." Thus I believe that in
the ministries of the Christian Church the Ascended
LORD stoops to me from Heaven, for grace and truth
come to me by JESUS CHRIST.

Here, then, we recognize the revelation given us of
our Ascended LORD as "the Head of the Body, the
Church." But another question arises in our mind:
How is the Body held in union with Him? And the
answer is this: By the indwelling of the Spirit of Life.
Look again at our natural body. We may see the
natural body at one moment a living organism, each
part fulfilling its proper function in obedience to the
dictates of the head, because a living spirit dwells
within. The next moment we may see the union of
action between the parts beginning to dissolve and the
members beginning to separate,—why? Because the
living spirit has departed and no longer dwells within.
And what the indwelling of my human spirit is to my
body, that the indwelling of the HOLY SPIRIT is to the
Catholic Church of CHRIST; and while the Church is
thus held in mysterious union with its Head, the
stream of Spiritual Life flows from that Head to all
His members and knits each to each, for "we, being

many, are one body in CHRIST, and every one mem·
bers one of another " (Rom. xii. 5).

This is the vision we have to face to-day, and it is
one which it is very difficult to grasp. What we need
to remember is, that the true view of the Church, as of
all other things, can only be obtained by considering
it on its *ideal* side. Take, for instance, family life,—
how seldom is its ideal realized! How often is our
conception of the Christian family as the sphere of
love and sympathy and ordered activities marred by
the human imperfections we find in it! It is the same
with human character,—when we look with unloving
criticism upon those around us, we see so much of
imperfection even in the best and holiest characters,
that we are in danger of falling into unholy cynicism
and losing all faith in our fellow-men! But if we look,
instead, at what is GOD's ideal for them, and regard
what (amidst many failures) they aspire and strive
to be, then we get the true view of humanity as
it shall be when it attains its true perfection in the
presence of GOD. So it is with the Church. There is
nothing more disappointing than the picture which it
presents at first sight to the student of history. Of
all the records which tell of man's littleness, there is perhaps none which records a more humiliating tale than
the page on which I find the history of the Church.
On one side it is indeed of the earth, earthy ; and yet
it lives on, disjointed, marred though it be, and at
this present time the Christian Church looks round
on all existing dynasties as being still in their infancy,
on all existing societies as being comparatively of
to-day, contrasted with her centuries of age. In every

generation, age after age, the hearts of the Church's children have trembled for her safety, and they have thought that the powers of the world were too mighty for her. But no,—like GOD's truth, GOD's Society lives on, ever dying, yet still living on from age to age, and through ever-recurring crises it will live on till the Coming of the LORD. Why? Because it has life only through union with the Ascended JESUS, and this union is maintained only by the indwelling of the HOLY SPIRIT. And so the expression so often used, "The Church does this or that," though in a sense it is true, is not the whole truth, for it sounds as if the Church were regarded as the delegate of an absent LORD, instead of as the instrument of a present LORD. And what is true is this: It is not the Church that baptizes those who come to the font; it is not the Church that absolves those who seek the ministry of reconciliation; it is not the Church that feeds those who seek the Heavenly Food of the Eucharist; it is not the Church that teaches the truth embodied in her creeds; it is JESUS, the Ascended One, Who thus acts on men through the ministries of His Body the Church. The one view presents to me something which comes between me and my LORD.—That I cannot do with! Away with it! The other view shows me my LORD drawing me near to Him through the instrument which He created as a means of contact with Himself. And thus I know, as I live my life within the bounds of the Catholic Church, that the Voice by which I am taught is the Voice of the Ascended JESUS, and the Hand by which I am dowered is the Hand of the Enthroned Head of the Church.

Fifth Reading.

1 PETER iii. 21, 22; TITUS iii. 4-7.

THE like figure whereunto even Baptism doth also now save us (not the putting away of the filth of the flesh, but the answer of a good conscience toward GOD,) by the Resurrection of JESUS CHRIST : Who is gone into Heaven, and is on the Right Hand of GOD ; Angels and Authorities and Powers being made subject unto Him.

But after that the kindness and love of GOD our Saviour toward man appeared, not by works of righteousness which we have done, but according to His mercy He saved us, by the Washing of Regeneration, and Renewing of the HOLY GHOST ; which He shed on us abundantly through JESUS CHRIST our Saviour ; that, being justified by His grace, we should be made heirs according to the hope of eternal life.

V.

THE REVELATION OF THE SYSTEM OF THE CHURCH.

IT may we well for us to pause a moment before going further in our meditations on the Ascended Life of our LORD, and to consider what is the point which in those meditations we have now reached.

We have seen that the Ascended JESUS has merited for us, by the obedience of His life on earth, consummated by the obedience of His death, the two great gifts of Truth and Grace. We have seen that what He merited for us on the Cross of Calvary He is perpetually claiming for us by His ceaseless intercession in Heaven, so that at this moment the gifts of Truth and Grace are being won for the sons of men by Him Who stands as our Interceding Priest before the Throne of GOD. We have seen Him as the Perfect Man receiving into Himself the fulness of Grace and Truth, in order that, as the Bountiful King, He may communicate those gifts to His people on earth and in Paradise. And we have seen that the great instrument He uses whereby to communicate to man the gifts of Truth and Grace, is His mystical Body, the Holy Catholic Church.

To-day another fact claims our attention in connec-

tion with this part of our subject, and it is this: that
in His Church the Ascended JESUS wills to give gifts
unto men through certain visible, tangible means.
The law of the Kingdom of GOD which thus comes
before our minds is the law of sacramental action,—
the law by which JESUS CHRIST has linked the gifts
He won for man to special, distinct, definite media,—
so that, if we wish to receive GOD's gifts, we must go
for them to the Living LORD, in the means of grace
which He has created, in order that through them He
may impart to us those gifts.

The passage of Holy Scripture which is placed at
the commencement of this Reading will serve as a
basis for our consideration of this subject. " The like
figure whereunto even Baptism," says S. Peter, "doth
also now save us,"—and then he goes on to explain
the nature of the salvation of which he is speaking:
" Not the putting away of the filth of the flesh, but the
answer of a good conscience toward GOD." He tells
us that Baptism is not merely an external cleansing,
but that it conveys an internal cleansing of the conscience. There is here a clear statement as to the
effect of Baptism, and an explanation of that effect,—
a statement as clear as words can make it,—" Baptism
doth also now save us, by the resurrection of JESUS
CHRIST: Who is gone into Heaven, and is on the
Right Hand of GOD; angels and authorities and
powers being made subject unto Him " (1 S. Peter iii.
21, 22). It is no unusual thing to hear people criti-
cise the expression, "Are you saved?" Those whom
I may call hypercritical Catholics shrink back from
the question, and say that it is one which cannot be

answered in this life; they imagine it to be presumptuous to speak of salvation as a present state, or of the baptized as in a state of salvation. Well, they must argue that with S. Peter! for here he distinctly says that salvation is a present state, and that the baptized (if they remain true to their baptism) are saved. And it behoves us to recognize a danger here, and to see that, as is too often the case, there lies beneath the criticism prompted by a narrow ecclesiastical spirit, not the rejection of what is thought to be Protestant presumption, but really the denial of a fundamental truth of Christianity. The whole postulate of the Christian life as assumed by Catholic theology is this: it is not the reaching forth to the hope of a salvation which may some day be attained; it is the living out of a salvation which now exists, from the starting-point of a life already saved. To be *in* CHRIST is to be saved, and by Baptism we are made members of CHRIST; for, as S. Paul puts it, "as many of you as have been baptized *into Christ* have put on CHRIST" (Gal. iii. 27); and therefore to be living in that union with CHRIST to which we are admitted by Baptism is to be in the present possession of salvation in CHRIST JESUS. We are taught to believe that a simple rite "ordained by CHRIST Himself," (and there is none simpler,) the pouring of water on the person who comes to be baptized, accompanied by the utterance of a certain formula of words, puts the recipient of the rite, if he is in a fit state to receive it, into a state of salvation. Whether he will always remain in it is another matter.

"Baptism doth now save us,"—these words are not

th ose of any modern theologian, they are not those of
the Prayer-book ; they were written by one who was an
Apostle of the LORD JESUS,—who companied with
Him "all the time that He went in and out among"
men, who was "with Him in the holy mount," and was
an eye-witness of His majesty (2 Peter i. 16–18), who
spake as he was "moved by the HOLY GHOST" (ver.
21); and the word he is bidden to say to you and
me is, "Baptism doth even now save us." Ay, but
how? why? Look you,—the Crucified One is the
Risen One ; yea, the Risen One is the Ascended One;
yea, the Ascended One is the Enthroned One,—you
see the steps, Resurrection, Ascension, Enthronization;
the gifts of GOD are His to distribute as He wills, and
He wills to give the grace of Regeneration whereby we
are born into the family of GOD, through the sacrament
of Baptism. Baptism saves us not of or by itself, but
because it is the means whereby the Ascended JESUS,
Who won salvation for us, and Who claims salvation
for us, wills to give to us the salvation which He has
won and is claiming ; it is the place where the Ascended
JESUS meets the sinner and enfolds him in His sacred
embrace, and makes him a child of GOD and an
heir of everlasting life. We are thus taking the sacrament of Baptism as a representative instance to illus-
trate this truth : that the gifts of Truth and Grace
flow to us from our Incarnate LORD through sacramental media, the means of grace which He has
ordained. But, remember, this is true not because it
is the *essential* condition of the bestowal of these gifts
by our LORD that He should give them through the
means of grace, but because He has revealed that it is

His Will so to do. Had He so willed He might have
given us all the gifts of GOD without the introduction
of any media, as we know He did reveal the truths
of His Gospel to S. Paul after His conversion. "I
certify you, brethren," says S. Paul, "that the gospel
which was preached of me is not after man; for I
neither received it of man, neither was I taught it, but
by the revelation of JESUS CHRIST" (Gal. i. 11, 12).
The Ascended JESUS might have revealed to each
soul the whole story of His life and death on earth,
and the full purpose of GOD's Will for that soul and
for the whole race of men, by immediate communication to man's intellect; He might have given all the
grace needed by each soul directly and immediately
to each soul by communion of spirit without the
instrumentality of any means of grace. We may go
further. We do not for a moment deny that our
Ascended LORD may and does give His gifts of grace
to man, if so He wills, without employing sacramental
media; we do not for a moment deny that He may
and does, if so He wills, reveal His truth to intellects
that have never been brought in contact with His
written Word. We do not forget that great utterance
of the master of Western theology: "The grace of
GOD is not limited to the sacraments of the Church."
No,—it is in grace as it is in nature. If GOD so will,
He may keep men in life even though they use not
the means which He gives to sustain life. Holy
Scripture tells us of certain cases in which He did
this, of Moses and Elijah, and of our LORD Himself
in the days of His flesh. (See Exod. xxiv. 18 and
xxxiv. 28; 1 Kings xix. 2–8; S. Matt. iv. 1, 2.) And

just so, wherever beyond the limits of the Church, and without the use of the sacramental media, I see beauties of character,—whether it be in the separated societies of baptized Christians around us, or amongst those who lack Baptism, such as the Society of Friends, or even amongst the ranks of heathendom,—I recognize those beauties of character as the gift of the Ascended JESUS, and I rejoice to know that through His mercy the living waters of grace overflow their channels on every hand.   Yet, after all, the fact remains that if we desire to receive the gifts won for us by our Incarnate, Crucified, Risen, and Ascended Saviour, we can only with certainty receive them by the application of the means created by Him through which to bestow those gifts.   Let us take an illustration which will be clear to all.   You will admit that GOD gives the knowledge of His truth through the medium of Holy Scripture.   This is a fact which no seeker after GOD will deny.   For if a man were to say that he wanted to learn GOD's truth, and therefore he would cast his Bible into the fire and demand a direct revelation from GOD to his soul, you would say that he was acting presumptuously in requiring GOD to give immediately what GOD has willed to give mediately, and no one could wonder if he went on in ignorance of the truth.   We cannot learn the truth of GOD without going for it to the Word of GOD.   Well, then, the truth of GOD comes to me through the means of a Book which was compiled by men, printed by men, bound by men, handed down by men from one to another; and if I want to receive into my intellect the truth which GOD has revealed in the Person of JESUS

Christ, I must approach with reverence to this Book of Life and study it. "Search the Scriptures," is our Lord's command, "for they are they which testify of Me" (S. John v. 39). The light of God's truth comes to me not immediately, by direct communication from Him, but mediately, through the medium of His Book. But notice, there are *two* great gifts to which we have access through the Incarnation: "*Grace and Truth* came by Jesus Christ.*" Why is it superstitious to believe that God's gift of grace is bestowed in accordance with the same law which He has laid down regarding His gift of truth? If it is an acknowledged fact that in order to obtain God's gift of truth we must come to His Book, surely it is no less true that in order to obtain His gift of grace we must come to His Sacraments? He *can* give grace immediately, but He has revealed to us that He *wills* to give it through sacramental channels.

In considering this subject, we will fix our thoughts on the two great sacraments ordained by Christ Himself, taking them as representative of all other means of grace.

The first thought that comes to us here is this: that if I am to be living in that abiding union with Jesus Christ which is the condition of my salvation and of my enjoyment of the blessings stored for us in His Kingdom, He must make me His own child. He reveals to me this fact, that if I want to be accepted of Him I must come to Him in the sacrament of Baptism, because Baptism is His own outstretched Hand, wherewith He waits to embrace all who draw nigh to Him therein. Let us take the case of some soul which has been awakened from a life of sin, and has begun to be truly sorry for the past, and truly desirous to do GOD's Will in the future,—what is to be its first step along the path of a new life? There are those who would say simply to throw itself on the mercy of GOD and believe that it is saved. But that is not the teaching of the Bible,—the first question for the Christian pastor or friend to put to such an one is: Have you been baptized? For there is just such a case recorded in the Bible, of a man who was very sorry for his sins, and very anxious to know GOD's Will, and to him the LORD's Word came by His messenger: "Why tarriest thou? Arise, and be baptized, and wash away thy sins, calling upon the Name of the LORD" (Acts xxii. 16). Ananias directs the penitent Saul to seek the Ascended JESUS in the sacrament of Baptism, because it is the means whereby our LORD embraces His elect and brings them into union with Himself. And it was precisely the same with the three thousand souls who were converted on the Day of Pentecost. To them S. Peter said, "Repent, and be baptized every one of you in the Name of JESUS CHRIST for the remission of sins, and ye shall receive the gift of the HOLY GHOST" (Acts ii. 38). Again, when Philip the Deacon spake to the Ethiopian eunuch of the salvation wrought out upon the Cross, it is evident that he must have pointed to Baptism as the means of becoming a partaker in that salvation, else what led the Ethiopian to say, "See, here is water; what doth hinder me to be baptized?" (Acts viii. 36). And what are the words of the LORD JESUS Himself before His Ascension? "He that

believeth and is baptized shall be saved" (S. Mark
xvi. 16).   That is to say, in the sacrament of Baptism
the Living JESUS Himself meets those who are fit re-
cipients of that sacrament, and by its means cleanses
them from their sins and makes them members of
His own family, "born anew of water and of the
Spirit." It is through the medium of Baptism that
the grace of Regeneration flows from the Ascended
JESUS to each member of His Church.

And as it is with the first sacrament, so it is with
the second.   The Ascended JESUS gives to those
whom He hath brought into union with Himself food
for the sustenance of their spiritual life.   He hath
prepared a table in the wilderness and given bread to
His people; and what is true of Him in every part of
His redeeming work is true here: "CHRIST is All, and
in All" (Col. iii. 11).   He is the Prophet, and yet He
is the Truth which He teaches; He is the Priest, and
yet He is the Victim which He offers; He is the
King, and yet He is the Gift which He bestows; He
is the Host, and yet He is the Very Food whereon He
feeds His guests.   He took into His Hands the bread
of earth which lay before Him, and said of it, "This
is My Body;" He took of the wine of earth, and
said of it, "This is My Blood."   For as the Church
is His Body, not by being changed into His actual
Humanity, but by being united to that sacred Humanity, as the Church is thus the continuation of His
life on earth,—so this great law of assimilation of the
creature with the Creator passes on farther still, even
to the depths of the vegetable kingdom; and He Who
takes you and me, poor children of dust as we are,

and makes us members of His mystical Body, takes
the bread and wine which we lay at His Feet, and by
the power of the HOLY SPIRIT lifts them into union
with Himself, so that "the Cup of Blessing which
we bless is the Communion of the Blood of CHRIST,
the Bread which we break is the Communion of
the Body of CHRIST" (1 Cor. x. 16). He Who died
for us on the Cross gives Himself to us as our
spiritual food and sustenance in the sacrament of the
Eucharist. "I am the Bread of Life" are His words
to us; nothing less precious than Himself can nourish
and develop our souls' growth; and as the sustenance
of our natural life depends on our receiving the bread
of earth which is the GOD-appointed means of its
support, so the sustenance of our spiritual life depends on our receiving Him Who is the Bread of
Life in the sacrament which He has created through
which to give us bread from Heaven. It is on the
fact of the Ascension of JESUS CHRIST that the
power of the Eucharist mystically depends. He
taught this twice while He was on earth; first in
the conversation with His disciples in the synagogue
at Capernaum (S. John vi. 60–64), and once more
in revealing Himself to Mary Magdalene after His
Resurrection: "Touch Me not." Why? "For I
am not yet ascended to My FATHER" (S. John xx.
17). It was but a transitory forbiddal,—with the
change from the risen to the ascended life of JESUS
it passed away,—and thus beneath the forbiddal
there lies the revelation of a promise: "When I am
ascended to My FATHER, then thou shalt touch Me;"
for it is the Ascended JESUS Who sheds the benedic-

tion of His Spirit upon the elements which, according to His command, we lay at His Feet; it is the Ascended JESUS Who has created the great mystery of the Eucharist; it is the Ascended JESUS Who comes to be present with us in that Sacrament of His love, and Who there feeds us with food convenient for us to the strengthening and refreshing of our souls. Thus, as in the sacrament of Baptism I know the joy of my LORD's embrace when He enfolds me in His everlasting Arms and makes me His child, so in the sacrament of the Eucharist I know the joy of His healing touch, the benediction of His loving Hand, as He stoops to me from Heaven. And what is true of these two sacraments is true of all other means of grace, for Sacramentalism is the system which permeates the whole Kingdom of GOD; and whether it be in what S. Augustine calls "the sacrament of Prayer," or in Confirmation, or in Absolution, that we seek Him, it is the Ascended JESUS Who gives strength unto His people; it is He Who gives His people the blessing of peace.

Thus, then, we learn to recognize the great law of spiritual life under which we live. We have no need to be ever painfully reaching forth to the attainment of our LORD's mystic embrace,—in Baptism (blessed be His Name!) that embrace is ours, and however fickle our love may be, His love to us is abiding:—

> "Our earthly friends may fail us,
>   And change with changing years,
> This Friend is always worthy
>   Of that dear Name He bears."

That baptismal embrace, by which He has brought us into union with Himself, is an act that cannot be repeated, any more than our natural birth can be repeated; for weal or woe it is ours; and as our human birth is an abiding blessing if we are true to the great laws laid down by GOD for the guidance of natural life, so our new birth is an abiding blessing if we are obedient to the laws revealed for the guidance of spiritual life. But if we set those laws at defiance it is an abiding woe; for as no one born into this world can by any possibility be unborn, so there is no possibility of undoing that new birth; it is "the children of the *Kingdom*" of whom our LORD tells us that some "shall be cast out into outer darkness."

But while it is true that we have no need to seek a second time that embrace whereby in Baptism He has united us to Himself, it is also true that to maintain that union there must be the response of our own free will to the act of His free love. *This* is necessary,— that we should willingly yield ourselves up to the inworking of His baptismal grace. This fact gives us the answer to a question that is not infrequently asked: Is conversion necessary, and necessary for all? Now, first, let us have clearly in our minds the meaning of the term Conversion. I mean by Conversion the surrender of my will to GOD in response to His love to me revealed in JESUS CHRIST. If this is so, and since will is free, and can only willingly be yielded after the power of volition is developed, Conversion *is* needful for all; for till the will is fully and freely yielded up to GOD the baptismal union with the Ascended JESUS remains in suspense. Therefore, if we would live in the knowledge of the powers of the regenerate life, it is essential that we should have given ourselves up in willing self-surrender to GOD. We see, then, that two things are necessary, for two wills have to be brought into harmony : if JESUS draws us to Himself as His saved children in Baptism, we must take Him to ourselves as our Saviour and King in Conversion ; if His Will has come out to us in Baptism, our will must go out to Him in Conversion. It is no denial of His sacramental action upon us to say that we must each take Him voluntarily as our own Saviour ; nay, the strongest ground the evangelist can plead in pressing the necessity of Conversion upon the sinner is this : He has saved you in Baptism ; now, therefore, respond to His love by newness of life.

This action of the will, then, in conscious self-surrender, is the first condition of our living a life true to our baptismal calling ; and, believe me, the reason that we see disappointing lives lived by so many baptized persons, is that this first step in the renewed life has been slurred over. It is a scandal to us as Catholic Christians that we should hear with aversion and regard with suspicion a word so consecrated in the theology of the Catholic Church as the term Conversion. Any one who studies the language of mediæval theology knows well that the necessity for Conversion occupies in it a prominent place which is too often denied to it in the so-called Catholic teaching of the present day. And the question which we have each and all to answer to ourselves is this : Saved by JESUS, and united to JESUS in Baptism, have I surrendered myself to Him in " the obedience of faith"? Have I, by a responsive act of my will, taken Him for my Saviour Who has taken me for His child? Am I really and truly trusting Him for all the blessings of the regenerate life, for daily cleansing, daily sustenance, daily guidance, daily protection? If the answer of our heart is: Yes,—with all my sins and shortcomings, with all the fickleness of my love and the fitfulness of my faith,—still I do know that my Beloved is mine and I am His!—then the consequence is certain; there must be peace in the soul. How can I live trusting in Him Who for me lived and died on earth, Who ever liveth to make intercession for me in Heaven, Who stooped to embrace me in Baptism and to place me in a state of salvation, and yet fail to know that peace of GOD which passeth all understanding? It must be so, for with conscious trust in the Ascended JESUS there comes the removal of fear and doubt; and having learned, by acts of self-surrender oft-renewed, again and again to take Him for my Saviour, my Prophet, Priest, and King, henceforth I live my life in conscious union with Him in that mystical society which is His Body, the Church. For I know that if I seek Him there He will surely meet me,—in Confirmation if need be; in Absolution if I am called to it; in continual Prayer and study of Holy Scripture; above all at His Table, in the dear sacrament of His love,—for in every means of grace I draw nigh, not to *it*, but to *Him*, as Ananias bade Saul come to be baptized, "calling on the Name of the LORD."

Such are the conditions under which we live our life; this is the vision of the Ascended JESUS revealed

to us to-day. With Stephen I look up steadfastly into
Heaven, and I see the Son of Man standing at the
Right Hand of God; but I see His Hands stretched out
to me on earth as He stoops to me in the ministries of
His Church, holding out to me His Word, His Sacraments, that I may through each means of grace receive
from Him the special gift that through each He gives,
the special grace that He sees I need. And this is
not a thing that once has been, like the Death once
died on Calvary, nor is it a thing that one day shall
be, like His Return and Appearance in Glory; this is
a present thing, a system in the midst of which we are
now living. O glorious vision! Verily "the lot has
fallen to me in a fair ground; yea, I have a goodly
heritage!" Truly "the tabernacle of God is with
men, and He doth dwell with them!"

Oh for faith to realize what God reveals as being
the actual condition of our life lived in union with
the Ascended Jesus in the holy Catholic Church!
There is nothing to distract our gaze from Him,
nothing supplementary to His work, nothing to take
from His All-sufficiency. On this height of our
spiritual Zion, like the Apostles on the Mount of
Transfiguration, we see nothing but Jesus only;
Jesus is the substance of every truth; Jesus is the
power of every sacrament; Jesus is the end of every
law of life. In the ministries of the Catholic Church
I hear but one Voice, the Voice of the Living Jesus;
I see but one Minister, "Who is set on the Right
Hand of the Throne of the Majesty in the Heavens;
a Minister of . . . the true Tabernacle, which the
Lord pitched, and not man" (Heb. viii. 1, 2).

Sixth Reading.

1 CORINTHIANS ii. 1-3 ; ACTS xviii. 9, 10.

AND I, brethren, when I came to you, came not with excellency of speech or of wisdom, declaring unto you the testimony of GOD. For I determined not to know any thing among you, save JESUS CHRIST, and Him crucified. And I was with you in weakness, and in fear, and in much trembling.

Then spake the LORD to Paul in the night by a vision, Be not afraid, but speak, and hold not thy peace : for I am with thee, and no man shall set on thee to hurt thee ; for I have much people in this city.

VI.

THE REVELATION OF THE DIRECTOR OF SOULS IN THE CHURCH.

OUR purpose in these Readings has been, so far, the consideration of the Christian Life as lived in varied visions of our Ascended LORD. And to-day we have to dwell on another of these revelations, without which the needs of our soul could not be fully met.

We have seen the Ascended JESUS stooping to us from Heaven, speaking to us with His own Voice, reaching out to us His own Hand, calling upon us to yield to His utterances the assent of faith and to His gifts the receptivity of faith. But what would it avail to bid one who is blind to open his eyes and gaze on the beauties of GOD's world, or to bid one who is paralyzed to stretch forth his hand and receive an offered gift? GOD must not only stoop to us from without in the Person of JESUS CHRIST and offer us His blessed gifts, but He must also work His Own wondrous work within us if we are to have that grace of receptivity whereby alone we are enabled to accept that which He offers. And therefore we have now to consider that aspect of our LORD's Ascended Life which represents Him as the Individual and Personal Guide of His people, leading them on with a direct and personal leading, and developing in them the power to apprehend His Truth and to lay hold on His Grace.

As the basis of our meditations on this subject, let us call to mind the circumstance alluded to in the passages of Holy Scripture which form the heading of this Reading. S. Paul is in a position of special perplexity; he is doubting whether he shall stay in Corinth, and continue his preaching there, or whether it is really (as it almost seems to be) a waste of time and strength. And in the midst of his perplexities, one night as he rests, the Ascended LORD appears to him, and gives him the direct and immediate guidance that he needs: "Then spake the LORD to Paul in the night by a vision, Be not afraid, but speak, and hold not thy peace; for I am with thee, and no man shall set on thee to hurt thee, for I have much people in this city" (Acts xviii. 9, 10). This may be taken as a representative instance giving us an insight into the true life of the regenerate. All GOD'S children are led step by step through life, by JESUS, their Ascended MASTER, in the power of the HOLY GHOST. This truth is one which it is important to hold as tenaciously as we hold the truth of the sacramental action of our LORD upon us. It has been sometimes imagined that these two truths are antagonistic, but it is not so; they are really complementary truths. Unless we are being acted on inwardly by the HOLY SPIRIT, we cannot accept the external guidance given in His Word and in His Church; unless we are being inwardly moved by the HOLY SPIRIT, we cannot lay hold on the grace offered us by our Ascended LORD in His wondrous Sacraments.

It is, then, through the indwelling of the HOLY
SPIRIT of GOD that the Ascended One acts upon each
one of us, guiding us with a personal guidance and
educating us with a personal education. JESUS, by
His Spirit, dwells in each one of His elect; He
teaches each intellect with a personal teaching; He
acts on each heart with a personal action; He moulds
each will with a distinct personal purpose. For we
must remember that, while it is true that GOD wills
that His children should be bound together in the
unity of the Body of CHRIST, it is also true that a uni-
form type of character is not a law of GOD's Kingdom.
" He telleth the number of the stars, and calleth them
all by their names " (Ps. cxlvii. 4), because each creation
of His embodies a distinct conception of the Divine
Mind. And it is the same with human character;
every individual soul embodies a distinct conception
of the Divine Mind, and so no two men, no two women
are formed in the same mould,—GOD breaks every
mould after He has formed one character,—and the
purpose of the Ascended JESUS, as He acts by His
Spirit on each of His elect, is to make each true to
Himself, to develop the individuality of each soul to
His ideal for it. Thus, while bringing us into His
Church to live our life under common influences of
teaching and sacraments, He at the same time so acts
upon us from within that we yet preserve our individuality. It is well for us to remember this; for the
undoubted tendency of unbalanced Christians is to
aim at producing a miserable uniformity of character.
They have one type of sanctity before their minds,
and they would compress and restrain every character

till all were conformed to that one type. But this
uniformity is not according to the Divine Ideal of
humanity, and therefore the Ascended JESUS holds
our hand through life, and deals with us not only by
influences from without, but by His Spirit from within;
He guides the conduct and moulds the character of
each, with a mighty manipulation, by His Spirit that
dwelleth in us. And the way in which our LORD
thus guides and moulds each soul, the way in which
He brings us to become responsive to His gifts of
truth and grace, is by acting supernaturally on every
part of our human being.

I. By His Spirit the Ascended JESUS illuminates
our intellect. It is the Reason which is the true
guide of life; every act we do ought to be an expression of the conviction of our mind. If it is the result
of any other motive-power,—if it is done, for instance,
in obedience to the dictates of mere emotional im-
pulse, or of ecclesiastical conventionality,—though it
were a right action if reasonably undertaken, yet for
us it is wrong, because in the one case it is a form of
self-indulgence, and in the other it is superstitious;
and it is self-indulgent or superstitious because it is
unreasoning. GOD has given us Reason to be to our
inner life what the eye is to our outer life, the guide
of our path, and as He acts on our reason in the
power of the HOLY GHOST He forms conviction in
the intellect. The truth that is uttered in His Word
and by His Church is made a reality to the intellect
by the revelation of His Spirit. We never really
apprehend any truth till we have learnt that truth
by the inner teaching of the HOLY GHOST; we may

think that we do, but most of us know, on the one
hand, what it is to hold a truth in a merely mechanical
way, and, on the other hand, what it is to have a vital
grasp of it; and we know that we can have no vital
grasp on any article of the Christian Faith until that
which is uttered by the Church or by the Scriptures
becomes to us the utterance of the Holy Spirit within
our own souls.   "No man can say that Jesus is the
Lord but by the Holy Ghost" (1 Cor. xii. 3); and so
the Ascended Jesus, while leading us into His Church
that there He may speak to us from without, at the
same time illuminates our minds from within; just
as, in the walk to Emmaus, He opened the minds of
His disciples to understand those truths with which,
by the hearing of the ear, they were already familiar.

II. Having, by the power of His Spirit, given conviction to the mind, our Lord next communicates
desire to the heart, filling it with the longing to
translate conviction into action and to make the life
an acted creed.   First in order He gives the knowledge of His truth; secondly, the love of His truth;
for mere knowledge can never issue in the life of
conformity to the Will of God.   Devils know God's
Will, and disobey it; men may know God's Will,
and yet fail to obey it, because their affections are
indifferent to what their intellect believes; God's children know His Will, and obey it, because through the
action upon them of the Spirit of Love there rises in
their hearts the love of that which He commands and
the desire to live in response to their knowledge of
His Will.

III. Having thus enlightened the intellect to appre-

hend His truth and kindled in the affections the
desire for conformity of life, the Ascended JESUS by
His Spirit impels and energizes the will; He leads
His children not only to know and to desire, but to
resolve. And the issues of life are in the will. It is
not enough for the intellect to be illuminated by the
Spirit, for the heart to be influenced by the Spirit,—
there must be more than this if we are to live in conformity to the known Will of GOD,—there must be
the action of the HOLY SPIRIT upon the will, leading
us to strong, definite resolve. What is resolution? It
is the gathering up of the whole power of the will, the
concentration of the whole being upon the purpose
of the will. This is where we are apt too often to
deceive ourselves; we make what we call resolu-
tions, for instance, at the end of our meditations, but
are they real? Where is the concentration of purpose? Where is the steadfast resolve of the will? Are
these not too often lacking? But presently the HOLY
SPIRIT of GOD makes us blessedly miserable under
the state of indecision into which we are drifting; a
light is thrown upon teaching with which we have long
been familiar, a voice speaks to our inmost being,—
"This is what you ought to do, this is what you ought
to give up,"—"Thine ears shall hear a word behind
thee, saying, This is the way; walk ye in it, when ye
turn to the right hand or to the left" (Isa. xxx. 21).
Then comes the desire that henceforth our life might
be not as it has been hitherto, but as we see it ought
to be, and the restlessness becomes intolerable, and
the will that has been wavering rises up and says, "I
will hesitate no longer; come what may, I will make

this sacrifice, I will take this step!" Then a mighty wave of resolve carries the soul onward, and the step is taken and the higher ground is gained.

So we learn that not only is the Ascended JESUS working wondrously upon us from without, as by His Spirit He reaches down through the Word and the Sacraments to us who are gathered into the unity of His Church, but that, also, He is working wondrously within us, one by one. No one knows that inner working of JESUS, not even those who are nearest and dearest to us,—nay, we are often scarcely conscious of it ourselves ; but it is a great fact in the Spiritual Kingdom that our Ascended LORD is, by His Own indwelling Spirit, ever moving us to draw nigh to Him in the path of holiness, and to live in realized union with Him in His Catholic Church ; that He is by His Spirit ever strengthening in us the power of receptivity, whereby we may know the truth He reveals to us in the Scriptures, and may receive the grace He communicates to us in the Sacraments. If this be true, then with what awful condescension does the Ascended JESUS indeed stoop to us ! If this be true, then with what awful reality are we called to live our lives under His personal direction ! Believe me, more than by any other being whose influence has been felt on our characters, have these lives of ours been moulded by the ceaseless direction of our Ascended LORD. Realizing this (and may GOD help each one of us to realize it !), let us pause to consider what the grasp of such a truth involves.   .

If JESUS, the Ascended One, is thus continually directing each soul by His Spirit, the great law of our life must be obedience to His Voice. It is the height of presumption not to respond to His Call; it is the height of wisdom to follow His guidance. And if we would yield ourselves implicitly to be moulded to the ideal of our Divine Director for us, our response to His vocation must be threefold.

First, we must respond *promptly*. We must not keep Him waiting; we must not give Him reason to repeat the complaint, "Behold, I stand at the door and knock." It is dangerous to delay the response to the Calls of JESUS,—we may, through the procrastination of a sluggish will, forfeit a high vocation; the light may wane, the Voice may cease to call, the opportunity given may be for ever withdrawn. Respond promptly to "thine unseen Guide." "Awake, thou that sleepest, and arise from the dead, and CHRIST shall give thee light!" (Ephes. v. 14). Secondly, we must respond *generously* and *fully*. We must have nothing to do with half-responses, with making our own terms with GOD. Say not (as Lot said of Zoar), "Is it not a little one?" but respond fully, remembering that reason demands it, that wisdom enjoins it. How much of the leanness of soul, the disappointment of spiritual experience, which we lament may be traced to the fact that our lives are but half-surrendered to the guidance of our Ascended LORD! We have not dared wholly to disobey Him, but we have lacked courage and generosity wholly to respond to His Call. Thirdly, we must respond *perseveringly*. It will not do to walk with Him a little way along the path of holiness in response to His Call, and then to turn aside; to do that is to forfeit the blessing to which He is leading us. No,—

> "Let a man contend to the uttermost
> For his life's set prize, be it what it will!"

Our LORD never sees reason to revoke any of His Calls; He never calls a soul to any state in which He does not will that soul to walk perseveringly. And if we would grow to the full knowledge of the bliss of a life lived in union with the Ascended JESUS, we must see to it that we respond to His vocation, not only with promptitude and generosity, but also with constancy, not taking back from Him to-day the sacrifice which, in obedience to His Call, we may have offered to Him yesterday.

If, thus, we give ourselves up to walk with JESUS, in obedience to the guidance of His Voice,—if, thus, we follow Him promptly, generously, perseveringly, Who, "when He putteth forth His own sheep, goeth before them,"—then, through the inner teaching of His HOLY SPIRIT, our grasp of truth and holiness shall become daily stronger; then, through the inner power of receptivity communicated to us by His indwelling Spirit, the grace that flows from Him through the Sacraments shall become to us increasingly an experienced joy; then with ever-growing thankfulness we shall bless His Holy Name, not only because He has created the green pastures of His Church wherein His sheep may rest, but also because, by His inner direction, He has taught us to know how rich those pastures are, and has given us grace to feed therein to the satisfaction of our souls. But, believe me, none

really knows the satisfaction of his mental needs
through the grasp of Christian doctrine,—none really
knows the satisfaction of his spiritual needs through
the grace of Christian Sacraments, — until the Ascended JESUS has inwardly revealed that doctrine to
his intellect, and till the Ascended JESUS has imparted
to him the power to feed with a thankful heart in the
pastures of the Catholic Church.

Seventh Reading.

EXODUS xix. 5, 6; 1 PETER ii. 4, 5, 9.

NOW therefore, if ye will obey My Voice indeed, and keep My covenant, then ye shall be a peculiar treasure unto Me above all people : for all the earth is Mine. And ye shall be unto Me a Kingdom of Priests, and an holy nation.

To Whom coming, as unto a Living Stone, disallowed indeed of men, but chosen of GOD, and precious, ye also, as lively stones, are built up a spiritual house, an holy Priesthood, to offer up spiritual sacrifices, acceptable to GOD by JESUS CHRIST. . . . But ye are a chosen generation, a Royal Priesthood, an holy nation, a peculiar people; that ye should show forth the praises of Him Who hath called you out of darkness into His marvellous light.

VII.

THE REVELATION OF THE CHARACTER OF THE CHURCH.

THE practical point we have been reaching in the course of the preceding Readings may be defined as this: that the life of the Regenerate, if lived under its true conditions, is a life of conscious realization of their union with the Ascended and Enthroned JESUS.

To-day we have to advance another step in our study of the LORD's Ascended Life, and to learn that His children are called on not only to live in conscious communion with Him, but also in conscious co-operation with Him in His blessed activities. The Ascended Life of JESUS has for its great object the realization in Time of the fruits of His Passion. Our great High Priest has passed into the Heavens, there to intercede for us, with the purpose of extending His Kingdom among men, and bringing them to live in loyal subjection to His beneficent sway; and in the Bible we are clearly taught to recognize this fact, that all who believe in the Ascended JESUS will respond to their knowledge of the meaning of His Ascension by doing their utmost to carry on His work in the world. Recall for a moment the exhortation addressed by the Angels to the assembled disciples as they lingered on

Olivet after their LORD's Ascension : "Ye men of Galilee, why stand ye gazing up into Heaven? This same JESUS, Which is taken up from you into Heaven, shall so come in like manner as ye have seen Him go into Heaven " (Acts i. 11).

The disciples are quick to apprehend the implied direction. Between the Departure and the Return of their LORD their posture is not to be that of the idle dreamer, of mere sentimental contemplation,—there is a great evangelizing work to be done amongst their fellow-men, there are valleys of degradation to be exalted, and mountains of pride to be made low, and the crooked ways of deceit and guile to be made straight, and the rough places of violence and wrong to be made plain, before the glory of the LORD shall be revealed and all flesh shall see it (Isa. xl. 4, 5), and they brace themselves at once for the task. "Then returned they unto Jerusalem from the mount called Olivet ; and they went forth, and preached everywhere, the LORD working with them, and confirming the word with signs following " (Acts i. 12 ; S. Mark xvi. 20).

We have seen that our Ascended LORD is as Priest for ever interceding, as King for ever going forth conquering and to conquer, seeking the establishment of His Kingdom upon the earth. We have seen that the instrument whereby He carries out His work on earth is His Body the Church, that in and through His Church He goes forth to establish His rule among men. Now we have to go on to consider a further revelation respecting the Catholic Church of CHRIST ; and it is that which is given us by S. Peter, as in

thought he turns back to the high calling set by
GOD before His ancient people, and points out to the
Christian converts of his own day that they are called
to rise up and possess those privileges to which their
spiritual ancestry had failed to respond.   " If so be ye
have tasted that the LORD is gracious," says S. Peter,
"to Whom coming, as unto a Living Stone, disallowed
indeed of men, but chosen of GOD, and precious, ye
also, as lively stones, are built up a spiritual house,
an holy Priesthood, to offer up spiritual sacrifices,
acceptable to GOD by JESUS CHRIST" (1 S. Peter ii.
3-5).   In this passage the Church is revealed to us as
a great Sacerdotal Society.   S. Peter's point is, that
our LORD, in dealing with individual souls, does not
simply meet their felt personal needs, but having first
poured into the soul the satisfaction of its felt wants,
He leads it on into a state of corporate union with
its fellow-Christians ; so that Christian after Christian,
having been sought and found by the Ascended JESUS,
is brought by the power of His Spirit into the organized community of His Church.   And this organized
community .s built up for one special purpose, as
S. Peter tells us, to be "a chosen generation, a Royal
Priesthood, an holy nation, a peculiar people ; that
ye should show forth the praises of Him Who hath
called you out of darkness into His marvellous light"
(ver. 9).   A Royal Priesthood !—that is, "a Kingdom
of Priests " (Exod. xix. 6), "to offer up spiritual sacrifices acceptable unto GOD."   It is important to grasp
as clearly as possible the fact of this sacerdotal character of the Kingdom of GOD, and the consequent
possession of a sacerdotal character by every member

of the Christian Church, in order to understand its connection with the work of the Christian worker, and of the life we live on earth with the life which JESUS lives in Heaven. Let us dwell on this subject a little more in detail.

Now, in the fulness of the meaning of the term, there is but One Priest. Our LORD JESUS CHRIST Himself is the One world-embracing, time-enduring Priest, — "He hath an unchangeable Priesthood" (Heb. vii. 24). The necessity for "priests many" exists only in a secondary sense; they are needed because their ministry is subject to the limitations of time and space : "They truly were many priests, because they were not suffered to continue by reason of death" (Heb. vii. 23). But since our great High Priest that is passed into the Heavens ministers there before GOD in the true Holy of Holies, and thence acts on each and all, through all space and time, in the power of the HOLY GHOST, He has a Priesthood which is not subject to change or withdrawal, but which is world-embracing and time-enduring; and if we would truly apprehend the sacerdotal teaching of the Christian religion we must start from the realization of this ruth, that there is but One Priest of Humanity, the Ascended JESUS. He, as Priest, stands within the true Holy of Holies ever offering before the Throne of GOD His Own acceptable sacrifice; He, as Priest, thence comes forth to man, ever acting on the souls in Paradise and on earth in the power of the HOLY GHOST. We find this double ministry towards GOD and towards man foreshadowed in the Jewish ritual of the great Day of Atonement; the High Priest went

first into the Holy of Holies, "not without blood,
which he offered for himself and for the errors of the
people" (Heb. ix. 7); but afterwards he came out to
"the Altar that is before the LORD," to sprinkle the
atoning blood upon it and the Tabernacle of the
Congregation, that the blood pleaded within the Veil
might become efficacious for the reconciling of all,
"because of the uncleanness of the children of Israel,
and because of their transgressions in all their sins"
(see Lev. xvi. 3, 11-20). And also thus the Priesthood
of JESUS CHRIST is operative not only in Heaven, but
on earth. But *how* does He come forth to execute
His Priestly work amongst men? We have seen that
it is through His Body, that great Society which He
holds in mystic union with Himself. And since the
Church is the instrument whereby the Ascended JESUS
carries out on earth His Priestly work, therefore on
the Church of JESUS there must be stamped a sacerdotal character. The Church has not an independent
priesthood, it does not merely carry on a work co-
existent with His; but it is the minister of His Priesthood whereby He acts on humanity.

We find this sacerdotal character of the Church of
CHRIST distinctly recognized by the Church itself. The
instance which most clearly illustrates this is that of the
form of authoritative absolution given in the Office for
the Visitation of the Sick. What are the opening words
of that form? "Our LORD JESUS CHRIST, Who hath
left power *to His Church* to absolve all sinners who
truly repent and believe in Him,"—to His Church,
not to the individual priest,—the priest acts as the
representative and organ of the Body of CHRIST,

G

but it is in the whole Body that the absolving power
resides, to the Body He gave "power to absolve
sinners." Those whom our LORD met in the Upper
Room at Jerusalem on the evening of the First Easter-
Day were not only the Eleven Apostles, it was the
company of those who believed on Him at the time
who were gathered together when their Risen Master
came to greet them. Upon them He breathed the
Breath, to them He communicated the Life that knit
them into One Body, and to that Body which He had
created He said, "Whosesoever sins ye remit, they
are remitted unto them." Thus, if JESUS is the great
High Priest of Humanity, it is through the collective
Society of His Catholic Church that He carries on
His sacerdotal work amongst men ; and so the Church
has a sacerdotal character, because she has to carry
out on earth the ministry of the Incarnate LORD
above. Does He stand and plead before the Golden
Altar in Heaven ? Then His Church must plead at
countless Altars on earth. Is He ever going forth in
the power of the Spirit to do His blessed work in the
souls of men ? She must, in the power of the Spirit,
do the same. And her activities are not simply a
repetition of His work ; it is indeed the same work
wherein she is active. She pleads on earth the same
sacrifice that He pleads in Heaven ; she carries on the
same blessed ministry as that which He carries on.
So that we learn that the great purpose of the existence
of the Church of CHRIST is, that through it the priestly
ministry of the Ascended JESUS becomes efficacious
among men. And what are the limits of the Church's
ministry ? Wide as are the limits of the intercession

of our great High Priest in Heaven, so wide are the limits of every uplifted Eucharist on earth ; as He intercedes for all, so His Church must intercede for all ; as His intercession embraces the whole family of man, so while she pleads for all she pleads for each. Further, as He died for all and acts on each and all in the ministries of His grace, so the Church's mission to souls must be all-embracing ; there must be none so fallen but she dares to seek among them such as shall be members of the mystic Bride of the Lamb ; there must be no region so remote but thither goes forth, in the energy of the HOLY SPIRIT, the GOD-commissioned Society seeking to bring home to the hearts and consciences of men the knowledge of their REDEEMER'S Passion.

We must pass on to another point which it is important to recognize. Since the Church bears, as we have seen, a sacerdotal character, it is clear that she must have properly constituted organs for performing her work. While it is true that, in a measure, the sacerdotal character rests upon each one of her children ("Ye shall be unto Me a kingdom of priests"); while it is true that each member of the Church performs that priestly function which is assigned to him, it is also true that the same function is not assigned to all, and that the sacerdotal power is communicated in varying degrees to each. The plenitude of sacerdotal power exists in the Episcopate ; each Bishop is in his Diocese the chief of that part of GOD'S flock, and is called to exercise in its fulness the priestly power. Not only can he minister the two great Sacraments of Baptism and the Eucharist, but to the Bishop alone is committed by the Head of the Church the power to administer Confirmation and to admit to Holy Orders ; so that in its *fulness* the priestly power, as communicated by our Ascended LORD to man, resides only within the limits of the Episcopate. In the Second Order of the Ministry (that which at the time the New Testament was written was called the Presbytery, but which, from the days of S. Ignatius in the second century, to our own times, has been called the Priesthood) the sacerdotal power exists in a more limited degree. The Priest cannot administer Confirmation, he cannot admit men to Holy Orders by Ordination ; there is a limit to the measure of the power committed to him ; it is his solemnly to bless the people in GOD's Name, to offer the Eucharist in union with his LORD's perpetual Intercession, to distribute the saving Food to those who come to Holy Communion, to bring the message of formal forgiveness to them that seek it,— but it is not his to exercise in every respect the same priestly functions that the Bishop does. At the same time, when we say that in the Priest the measure of the sacerdotal power is limited, we are not denying the reality of that measure which is granted to him. In the Diaconate the measure is still more limited, but yet it is real, and it exceeds that which is committed to the laity. Precisely the same law holds good as regards the whole Body of the regenerate ; there is a sacerdotal character imprinted on every member of it, for the Head is CHRIST ; and because CHRIST is the One true Priest, we are members of a priestly Being, and a measure of His Priesthood must

rest on every member of His Body, however insigni-
ficant. But the priestly power of the lay members of
the Church is still more limited than the measure
committed to the Deacon; it is not exercised in the
Congregation; it is to be used by means of the quiet
exercise of holy influence, and by lying low before
GOD, in secret or before the altar, in heartfelt intercession. Yet in its measure the sacerdotal power of
the Christian laity is real; though to assert its reality
is not to say that no distinctive Office is committed to
the Priesthood, any more than to assert the reality of
that Office is to deny that the *plenitude* of priestly
power does exist in the Episcopate alone. Each of
His members is placed by the Ascended JESUS in that
special position in which can best be exercised the
distinct measure of His Priesthood that is committed
to that one member. The Bishop in its plenitude,
the Priest and Deacon in more and more limited
measure, and the lay person under still greater restric-
tions, all exercise the same ministry; they are the
different organs of the one priestly Society, just as in
the natural body there are different organs, such as
the eye, the tongue, the hand,—and yet in each case
it is the whole body which acts and fulfils the purpose
of its existence under the direction of the head. We
are "a royal priesthood, an holy nation, a peculiar
people," that by us, as by a chosen instrument, the
Ascended JESUS, Who pleads for men in Heaven,
may do His work among men on earth. When we
have laid hold on this truth, we can see how intimate
is the connection between His Ascended Life in
Heaven and the work of His Church on earth, for

our whole life on earth is nothing less than a life of
co-operation with Him,—we share the longings of His
human Heart, we share the activities of His celestial
Life.

Thus there comes before us a great law of life. We
are consecrated to be priests unto GOD; we are called
with a high vocation, and that high vocation implies a
grave responsibility. It is our bounden duty to be
responsive to our priestly calling by the fulfilment,
each in our measure, of our priestly work. We have
seen that that work is twofold,—it is a work of intercession and a work of active toil. True it is that
some members of the Body of CHRIST are called
specially to the one, and some are called specially to
the other, part of the sacerdotal Office which it exer-
cises; yet in the most active life there should be some
measure of intercession, and in the most interceding
life there should be some active interests. Some are
called apart,—and it is a blessed call!—by sickness;
or if not entirely separated from active life, yet by
weakened health or an overwrought nervous tempera-
ment it is made clear to them that it is not the Will
of the Head of the Church that their service should
be that of busy toil. But the very withdrawal from
the sphere of active work is in itself a vocation to the
life of intercession, and this is the highest office of
the Christian Church. It is the special work of that
vast portion of the Church which has passed into
Paradise. The whole Church has a priesthood unto
GOD, and those who have passed within the veil share
in its sacerdotal character and vocation; but their
special work is that of intercession, and whilst we have

to go forth and fight the LORD's battles, they, like
Moses on the mount of old, hold up hands of prevailing intercession. There are few thoughts which
give to the Christian worker greater hope or greater
courage for his toil than the realization of this splendid verity of the intercession of the Saints of GOD in
Paradise, and also on earth, for they who are privileged
to be called to bear the cross of weakness or suffering
can anticipate here and now the life of intercession
which is the special work of those in Paradise. Yet
even on the lives of those who are called to active
service in the Church of GOD the obligation of intercession still rests. What is to be said of the Priest
who is ever ready to work hard amongst his people,
but who never secures time to plead with GOD for the
souls committed to his charge? What of the mother
who is always engaged in active ministries for her
children, but never bears them on her heart in the
Presence of GOD in prayer? What of the Sunday-
school teacher, ever active in looking up the children of his class, careful in preparation, systematic in
teaching, but who never kneels in prayer before GOD
for those to whom he carries His message? Must
one not say that the life is wrongly regulated,—that
the highest obligation of the Priest, the Mother, the
Teacher, was unrecognized? Woe to the Christian
worker who is content to be ever coming from GOD
to his fellow-men in the ministries of active toil, but
who passes not back from them to GOD in earnest
and continual intercession. This, then, is the first
aspect of our sacerdotal calling : by our Baptism into
CHRIST we are consecrated,—some almost exclusively,

some in a very limited degree, but all in some measure,
—to be intercessors with GOD for our brethren.

But we have said that our priestly calling has a twofold aspect, and we must pass on to the consideration
of the second part of the one ministry. This involves
the recognition of a truth which men too often fail to
realize; and that is, that the extension of our LORD's
influence among men, the extension of His Kingdom
upon earth, depends absolutely on the co-operation
of His people with Him in His toil for souls. No
nation has ever been converted to Christianity without
the toil and endurance of the missionary; no soul,
except, perhaps, Saul of Tarsus, has ever passed from
darkness to light in the knowledge of the truth except
as that truth came to him through the lips of a brother
or a sister in CHRIST. It is only as the knowledge of
the truth passes from mind to mind through the continual active service of Christian men and women
that the fruits of the Passion are reaped upon earth
and the Ascended JESUS is known and served worthily
by the souls for whom He died. It is,—is it not?—
a fearful and yet a splendid responsibility which rests
upon those who have learned to face their lives in
the light of this fact: that CHRIST has brought us
into union with Himself in His Church for this very
purpose, that He may make us His messengers to our
brethren; that to each one of us the Voice of the
Ascended One speaks with no uncertain sound,
"Let him that heareth say, Come!" (Rev. xxii. 16,
17). We are not fully responding to the Ascended
Life of JESUS, not fully realizing our standing as
members of the Catholic Church, not fully rising to

the obligations of our position as baptized Christians, if we are not by earnest prayer, but also by active endeavour, interceding, seeking, yearning, striving, for the conversion of sinners, for the extension of the Kingdom of Jesus Christ. It is a question which it behoves each one of us to put to ourselves : What am I doing for the salvation of the souls for whom my Lord died, and for whom He now pleads in Heaven? What am I doing for the conversion of sinners; what am I doing for the extension of the Catholic Church?

And if we are to respond aright to this high vocation, it can only be at the cost of self-sacrifice. There is no other way. Did not our Lord reveal that sacrifice was a condition of the fulfilment of His ministry by the toil and disappointment of His own Life, by the agonies of His Own Death? The Heart of Jesus Christ was filled by a great longing; He saw mankind lying in that which is called in the Bible "poverty," that is, sin,—He saw them wrapped in that degradation and sorrow and misery which are the consequence of sin; His compassionate Heart yearned for their salvation, for their elevation to the true position of humanity, the position of the children of God. And He left the unutterable bliss and perfect satisfaction and dignity of His Home,—"Though He was rich, yet for our sakes He became poor" (2 Cor. viii. 9). He passed from the Kingly Palace of Heaven to the poor Stable of Bethlehem, to the cottage home, to the carpenter's shop, thence out into the world to a life of homelessness, and of absolute dependence on the alms of others; and still further, to

the degradation, the pain, the anguish, of the Cross,—
that by His unstinted self-sacrifice He might minister
effectually to the needs of fallen men.   And it is His
priesthood that we have to carry on; we are where
He once was, amid a sin-stricken race, not yet where
He is, in the bliss of Heaven ; and we can only fulfil
our mission, as we go forth to live and toil with Him
among men, by self-sacrifice.   To each of us the Call
of Jesus is ever sounding, bidding us give up whatever holds us back from earnest living and generous
toil.   To one it comes as it did to Abraham : "Get
thee out from thy country, and from thy kindred, and
from thy father's house, . . . and I will bless thee, . . .
and thou shalt be a blessing" (Gen. xii. 1, 2); it is
the call to life in a religious community.   To another
the call is not thus to come apart from the world,
but to devote the life to active work in the world
amongst the fallen and the ignorant.   Mayhap the ties
of home-life have been severed ; mayhap no duty makes
clear the place or form of ministration ; then comes
the Call of the Ascended Jesus, pointing to the places
where vast multitudes of souls are massed together
who spiritually know not their right hand from their
left,—to our great cities, our ports, our camps, our
collieries,—and bidding the one whom He has set
free to be His messenger to go out and spend and be
spent in the service of His poor.   And there is another
call that is quite as clear, a call as high and noble as
any that can be named,—the call to work within the
sweet seclusion of the Christian home, and so to live
in that God-appointed sphere that each home may be
a fount of blessing, —the fresh springs of holy influence

permeating it and nourishing beauties of character in all its members, and then flowing out from it on every hand until the waste places round about become green and fertile as the garden of the LORD. In the community, in the world, in the home,—it matters not where the work is done,—but that a call to real, definite work for GOD, where and as He wills, sounds sooner or later in the ears of every true believer, is a certain fact in the Christian life.

Here, then, is our lesson to-day. The true way of expressing my faith in the Ascended JESUS, the true way of showing my gratitude to Him for all the benefits that He hath done unto me, is to do all that in me lies, both by earnest prayer and by active toil, to make His blessed Name known upon earth, and to extend the bounds of His glorious Kingdom,—it is to go on my way with words of self-oblation on my lips: LORD, what wilt Thou have me to do? where wilt Thou have me to be? "LORD, I will follow Thee whithersoever Thou goest." "Surely in what place my LORD the King shall be, whether in death or life, even there also will Thy servant be" (S. Luke ix. 57; 2 Sam. xv. 21).

Eighth Reading.

HEBREWS x. 9–13 ; 1 CORINTHIANS xv. 25.

THEN said He, Lo, I come to do Thy Will, O GOD. . . .
By the which Will we are sanctified through the offering
of the Body of JESUS CHRIST once for all. And every
priest standeth daily ministering and offering oftentimes
the same sacrifices, which can never take away sins : but
this Man, after He had offered one sacrifice for sins for
ever, sat down on the Right Hand of GOD : from henceforth expecting till His enemies be made His footstool.

For He must reign till He hath put all enemies under
His Feet.

VIII.

THE REVELATION OF THE DIVINE EXPECTANCY.

WE have been endeavouring in these Readings to learn what are the revelations of the Ascended Life of our LORD, and of its bearing upon our own life as Christians, which are granted us in the light that streams from the open Heavens at His Ascension. We have seen Him, first, as the Ideal Man, revealing the ideal state of manhood as He takes His place on the Right Hand of GOD. Secondly, as the Interceding Priest, pleading for His people the sacrifice of Himself. Thirdly, as the King of Glory, claiming the right to give the gifts of GOD unto men. Fourthly, as the Head of the Church, through the organism of His mystical Body extending to every member the fulness of life that is in Him. Fifthly, as the LORD of the Sacraments, through means of grace which are His Own creation giving us from His Own Lips and His Own Hand the gifts of truth and grace. Sixthly, as the Individual and Personal Guide of His people, developing each character and directing each life with an immediate personal guidance. And seventhly, as the great Evangelizer, animating His servants with fervent love for souls and generous longing to extend His Kingdom at whatsoever cost to themselves.

Now, there is one more amongst the many aspects of the Ascended Life of JESUS upon which I desire to dwell within the compass of these Readings ; because it seems to me to teach in a wondrous manner the secret of Perseverance, and I know that perseverance in responding to the revelations of GOD is the yearning of every loyal heart.

The vision, then, which comes before us to-day is that of the splendid Patience of the Ascended JESUS. He stands before us in His Heavenly as in His earthly life as the embodiment not only of all active but also of all passive virtues, the One perfect Character, the Ideal of Manhood, in Whom we find our Ensample not only in all noble activities, but also in all the majesty of hopeful forbearance and quiet waiting. "This Man, after He had offered one sacrifice for sins for ever, sat down on the Right Hand of GOD : from henceforth expecting till His enemies be made His Footstool." "From henceforth expecting!" What a wondrous revelation is here presented to us of the Ascended Life of JESUS CHRIST, as it is set before us in the Word of GOD, not under the aspect of a life of fruition, but of a life of expectation! For eighteen centuries and more has the Incarnate JESUS been set at the Right Hand of the Eternal Godhead ; and still, though nigh upon nineteen hundred years have rolled away since He withdrew from this world after accomplishing His great mission, the purpose of that mission remains unfulfilled. Yet through all these centuries of time, through all the strange vicissitudes of the history of his Church, our LORD, in calm, blessed hopefulness, has been living

a life of confident expectation, awaiting the pre-
destined hour of His triumph,—"From henceforth
expecting."

Surely this aspect of the Ascended Life of our
LORD is one which is not frequently enough dwelt
on in the meditations of Christian people. We do
not readily think of that Life as one of patient anticipation, but rather as one of restful attainment, of
the fulfilment of desired ends. That it is not so, we
shall see if we consider for a short space two revelations of the purpose of His ministry on earth as
they are given to us in the Scriptures. We are told
there that the purpose of the work of JESUS CHRIST
amongst men,—of His Incarnation, His Passion, His
Resurrection, His Ascension, His perpetual Intercession,—is the realization of His Eternal Ideal of
the Church. Back in the deep depths of the everlasting past, the thought of the Church in her fair
beauty as the Bride of CHRIST, filled the Mind of
the Eternal, and was a delight to the Heart of GOD.
Ideally the Church is a Society possessing four distinctive marks: 1. The mark of perfect unity: the
Church should perfectly manifest, as in a mirror, the
Unity of the Triune GOD. 2. The mark of perfect
sanctity: each member is to be holy and without
blemish, conformed to the image of the Son of GOD.
3. The mark of undying continuity: the Church,
which is created to be "the Bride, the Lamb's Wife,"
is to live on age after age, unmarred by time, in the
beauty of perpetual youth. 4. The mark of Uni-
versality: the Church should embrace within its
wide domain all nations and kindreds and peoples

H

and tongues. That is to say, the Church, regarded on its ideal side, is to be One, Holy, Apostolic, Catholic.

But, if the course of this world's history were to end to-day, what, of all grand conceptions of the human heart, would have proved after eighteen centuries of endeavour to be so vain and unattained an ideal as the conception of the Christian Church? The Ascended Jesus looks upon her from Heaven to-day, and sees her unity broken; He looks upon her from Heaven to-day, and sees her sanctity lacking; He looks upon her from Heaven to-day, and sees her apparently tottering as with the decrepitude of age; He looks upon her from Heaven to-day, and sees vast portions of the world lying utterly beyond her pale, while within many of the kingdoms where Christianity is professed her influence over the majority is merely nominal, and at the present time we see nation after nation rising in revolt against CHRIST and His Church. And yet,—though, after all these nineteen centuries of toil and prayer and earnest longing, the conception of His Mind for the Church is frustrated and unrealized,—there is no disappointment in His Sacred Heart, no cessation in His enduring ministry; He is waiting, expecting the dawn of that pledged day which, though it tarry long, will surely come; waiting till at last He shall see the "New Jerusalem prepared as a bride adorned for her husband," dwelling with Him in His Eternal Home.

Or again, if we take the thought of a second purpose of the ministry of JESUS, a second longing of

His Sacred Heart,—His longing for the conversion
of all men.   For all He died upon the Cross ; the sins
of all He bore in His Own Body to the Tree ; the
salvation of all is by Him wrought out : " Behold the
Lamb of GOD, Which taketh away the sin of the
world " (S. John i. 29).   And as for all He died, so
for all He pleads ; and as for all He pleads, so to all
He commands that the message of His redeeming
love be carried : " Go ye into all the world, and
preach the Gospel to every creature " (S. Mark xvi. 15).
And yet, at the present time, what a failure, looked
at as a great saving ministry, does the work of JESUS
CHRIST appear !   After nearly nineteen centuries of
time, the majority of the sons of men are yet ignorant
that a Saviour was ever born upon this earth, or died
for their sins upon the Cross, or lives to plead for
them in Heaven,—at this moment two-thirds of the
human race are living in the darkness of heathenism.
What, even, is the position of so-called Christian
nations ?   Is it not true that in our great centres of
population in England a large majority of the sons
and daughters of foil are living in a state as practically
heathen as that of any tribe in Africa or India ?   Is
it not true that numbers of our fellow-countrymen are
leading utterly godless lives,—the knee never bent, the
lips never uttering a prayer, GOD'S Day unhonoured,
His House neglected, His Book unreverenced, His
Claims denied,—living as though they had no eternal
future for which to prepare, no sinful past for which
to seek forgiveness, no GOD-created nature to be
trained and sanctified in the living present ?   What
thinking man can look at the population of Christian

England to-day, after all the evangelizing work that has been done up and down throughout her limits, and deny that, so far as working out a national salvation goes, the whole thing seems like a baseless hope?

And yet He wearies not. Confidently and ceaselessly for all He intercedes; with all, in the power of the Spirit, He still strives; yearning for the salvation of all, His command still rings out: "Go ye into all the world, and preach the Gospel to every creature." For through the thwarting of the present, He lives in anticipation of the certain triumph of the future, as at GOD's Right Hand He waits, "From henceforth expecting till His enemies be made His Footstool."

Now what is it that underlies this magnificent perseverance of the Ascended JESUS in His mediatorial ministry throughout the ages? What, but the blessed expectancy of hope which beats so strong in His Sacred Heart! Here, then, we find the secret of perseverance for each one of us, for "as He is, so are we in this world" (1 S. John iv. 17). The secret of our perseverance must be the power of Hope,— "We are saved by hope," says S. Paul (Rom. viii. 24). And what is hope? Hope is that virtue which lives in the promise of the morrow, not in the failure of to-day,—which fastens on that which shall be, not on that which is;—it is that virtue which through to-day's defeat reaches forward to to-morrow's triumph, and in the sorrows of the sowing-time anticipates the joy of the eternal Harvest-Home. If we fail in perseverance, whether in our outer or our inner life, the failure is due to the lack of hope, and of patience, the child of hope. For instance, take the growing unsettlement of the ecclesiastical mind to-day; why do we see men so shaken in their allegiance to their own branch of the Catholic Church, that both in the Churches of the Roman obedience on the Continent and in our English Church at home the strange sight is seen of Roman Christians seeking in English Christianity, and of English Christians seeking in the Roman Communion, that satisfaction which they have failed to find in their own? Whence comes it, but from this cause?—they who live long under obedience to one system become conscious of its shortcomings and defects; they see in the reality of that portion of the Church with which they are connected a painful contrast to the ideal Church which is present to their imagination; then after a time their dissatisfaction finds expression in an effort (such as the great Oxford movement in our own Church, or that with which the name of Lacordaire is associated in the Church of France) to bring the existing Church into fuller correspondence with our ideal of it. And because the effort is not at once successful, because the ideal remains unrealized and the aspiration for better things seems to be baffled, men lose heart and allow themselves to become dissatisfied with the position in which GOD has placed them; and instead of in quietness and confidence expecting till the Day of Fruition, they pass, in the unrest of hopeless impatience, from one Communion to another, seeking that which cannot be found here and now, a perfect Church on earth.

Again, why is it that thinking minds at times totter
and reel in their allegiance to the Faith of CHRIST?
Men look round on Christendom as it is after all these
centuries of Christian influence, and the state of things
they see there is so perplexing that he must be blind
who does not see or foolish who does not feel the
power of that perplexity.   Little children are born
and start in life without, as it seems, the shadow of a
chance; dwelling in homes of ignorance and sin, they
are nurtured in vice, trained in iniquity; from their first
consciousness the moral sense is warped; they pass
to manhood and live the life of the social outcast;
they die without apparently having had one chance of
amendment of life!   It is indeed an awfully perplexing thing to ponder upon the ideal of Christianity, and
then to contemplate the reality which is now presented
to our view.   Not long since one of the best-known
amongst the assailants of Christianity in the present
day remarked, after visiting the great gun-factories on
the Tyne, "You say CHRIST came to make peace on
the earth, to teach men to beat their swords into
ploughshares,—and one of the chief trades of your
Christian country is to carry to its highest development the art of manufacturing weapons of destruc-
tion!"   If we were indeed to expect the ideal of
Christianity to be realized under present conditions;
if our LORD had not told us that, while the ideal was
peace, the reality was to be that "nation shall rise
against nation, and kingdom against kingdom" (S.
Matt. xxiv. 7); if He had not foretold that the course of
the Christian Church, begun so confidently, would end
in seeming defeat,—"When the Son of Man cometh,

shall He find faith on the earth?" (S. Luke xviii. 8);
if He had not, in tenderest love, prepared us for this
apparent failure,—it is hard to see how the faith of a
single thinking man could have stood firm unto the end.

But He *has* told us, that before the end comes
there awaits the human race a great crisis.   The
conflict may be long, and for a time perhaps the
issue may seem doubtful or may look like sure defeat.
But, as Tennyson puts it, "Through every age one
growing purpose runs," because all the reins of this
world are gathered up into the Hand of the LORD
of History, the Ascended JESUS, Who guides its life,
by overruling it, to the accomplishment of His Own
purposes.   And at last, when the fulness of time is
come, His enemies shall be made His Footstool, and
the day of seeming defeat shall issue in glorious
victory.

And the same principle applies to our own inner
spiritual life.   How hard it is to persevere in true
Christian living!   At the outset of our Christian life
we have the simplest conception of what it means,—
all we have to do, we think, is to give up what is
wrong and to do what is right, to seek the grace of
GOD through His appointed means of grace, and then
all will be well.   We go forth to live our life in the
fulness of our purpose, and for a time, it may be, all
is comparatively easy; but this is because GOD, in
His mercy, deals with us as with very babes.   As we
press on along the narrow way we find that, instead
of the calm, unbroken ascent to the Celestial Mount
of which we dreamed, the Christian life is a fight,—
and not only so, but that it is a fight in which we

often fail, in which we are continually baffled. We strive, we pray, we agonize to conquer self and sin, and we don't conquer; or if we think we do, and that at least one difficulty is overcome, in a little while the old sin that we believed to be dead rises up and shows that it was only dormant, and the fight begins all over again. Or it may be that GOD shows us some beautiful ideal of character; He shows us what we might become if we were true to ourselves and to the possibilities of our regenerate nature, and we recognize that this is the ideal for us which is ever before the Mind of our Ascended LORD and is the longing of His Sacred Heart. Oh, how we long for that beauty of character! how we·reach forward to the attainment of that ideal! And yet the more we strive after the beauty of holiness, the more conscious we become of our deformity in unholiness. It seems as if the sustained effort, the ceaseless striving after better things, only made sin more apparent and more really active; and we are tempted (Who has not at some time been overcome by the temptation?) to yield to the paralyzing effects of spiritual depression and give up the weary struggle. "It is all in vain," we think, "trying to reach those heights of holiness that I see others reach: it is not in me to go on leading a life of meditation and prayer and self-control, trying to bear the yoke of CHRIST and to fight His battle, and yet growing none the better, but, as it seems to me, rather the worse! I shall give it up." Ah! but we forget that GOD sees that we need the discipline of defeat; that, in His wise love for souls, He permits all this temptation and failure because there is no other way of training us in that patience and hope whereby we may be conformed to the likeness of the Ascended JESUS. It is very wonderful how our LORD dwells in the Book of Revelation on the patience of the saints,—how Patience seems to be singled out amongst all other graces as the crowning beauty of His saints,—"Here is the patience of the saints" (Rev. xiv. 12, and xiii. 10. See also chaps. ii. 2, 3, 19, and iii. 10). And the meaning of the Greek word is literally *continuing under ;* it means that dogged plodding on under difficulties and in spite of hindrances which is the only means of progress in the spiritual life; not being in haste, but content to go on struggling and falling, and beginning over and over again, "expecting till" He gives success when and as He wills. And then there is the lesson of Hope; we have to learn never to despair, never to give in, but to go on trusting Him through everything, hoping against hope, crying out with Job, "Though He slay me, yet will I trust in Him!" (Job xiii. 15), expecting to triumph in the end, though He may keep us waiting perhaps all our life for the victory. He sees that we need the length of the conflict for our sanctification; that we, as the soldier on many an earthly battle-field, must continue to fight, through all the vicissitudes of the weary day, and only when the evening shadows fall will victory prove we have not fought in vain. And so we learn that the secret of perseverance, whether under the external trials of evangelistic toil or of ecclesiastical defect, or through the sore discouragements of our own spiritual life, is this: ever to keep our gaze fixed on Him Who, seated at the Right Hand of GOD, waits in the serenity of His divine patience, "From henceforth expecting till His enemies be made His Footstool."

One other thought comes before us as we con template this vision of the Ascended LORD, and to those who love Him there can be none more attractive.

How wonderfully may we enter into sympathy with JESUS if we are content to live this life of expectation! We crave for fruition, and fruition shall indeed be ours when the Mediatorial Reign shall be over and the LORD Himself shall enter on the full fruition of His redeeming work. But our union with Him now is the shared experience of patient waiting, of quiet confidence, of hopeful expectancy. One day shall come the realization of our most magnificent conceptions, the full satisfaction of the deepest longings of our souls. But His Word to us in the present is not "Blessed are they who rejoice in fruition," but "Blessed are they who hunger and thirst;" and as He, the Ascended JESUS, in His great love for souls, is ever, even in His Heavenly Life, hungering and thirsting for their salvation, so this is our beatitude now,—not to be rejoicing in ideals realized, but to be waiting patiently, in union with Him, for their realization, looking beyond the disappointment of the present to the sure satisfaction of the future, when "the times of refreshing shall come from the presence of the LORD, and He shall send JESUS CHRIST, . . . Whom the Heaven must receive until the times of restitution of all things" (Acts iii. 19-21).

GOD grant, to you and me, grace thus to live the life of blessed expectancy in union with our Ascended LORD! For they who thus wait upon GOD shall "go from strength to strength, until unto the GOD of Gods appeareth every one of them in Zion!" (Ps. lxxxiv. 7)

Ninth Reading.

St. Luke xxiv. 52, 53; Revelation v. 11-13.

AND they worshipped Him, and returned to Jerusalem
with great joy : and were continually in the Temple,
praising and blessing GOD.

And I beheld, and I heard the voice of many angels
round about the Throne, and the beasts and the elders :
and the number of them was ten thousand times ten
thousand, and thousands of thousands ; saying with a
loud voice, Worthy is the Lamb that was slain to receive
power, and riches, and wisdom, and strength, and honour,
and glory, and blessing. And every creature which is
in Heaven, and on the earth, and under the earth, and
such as are in the sea, and all that are in them, heard I
saying, Blessing, and honour, and glory, and power, be
unto Him that sitteth upon the Throne, and unto the
Lamb for ever and ever.

IX.

THE REVELATION OF THE JOY OF CHRISTIAN WORSHIP.

WE saw in our last Reading that the secret of our per-severance amidst the discouragements of the spiritual life, in union with the magnificent patience of our Ascended LORD, is the grace of Hope. To-day we learn from what is recorded of the Apostles imme-diately after the Ascension of their LORD, that the secret of the joy which is the great attraction of true Christianity is this: that the Christian Life is one of perpetual homage rendered to Him Who is both GOD and Man,—in Whom our humanity attains its ideal perfection by being taken into union with GOD,—the Incarnate Word, the Ascended JESUS CHRIST.

S. Luke ends his Gospel with the words: "And they worshipped Him, and returned to Jerusalem with great joy, and were continually in the Temple, praising and blessing GOD." The Apostles, and pro-bably some others of the disciples of JESUS, had been with Him for a little while on Mount Olivet. The moments spent there were comparatively few in number, but so much had been concentrated into them that (as often happens in our spiritual experi-ence) this short space of time formed a crisis never to be forgotten in the lives of those disciples. For there, on the heights of Olivet, they had gazed on their Ascending SAVIOUR; they had listened to His parting words; they had seen His loving Hands uplifted in blessing; they had watched Him as He went up, till the cloud, which is ever in the Bible the sign of the Divine Presence, received Him out of their sight, and they knew that He "was passed into the Heavens" beyond the ranks of angels and archangels, till, in the very Presence Chamber of the Eternal, He should be seated at the Right Hand of the Majesty on High. And that departure, the thought of which had not long before awakened in them a selfish sorrow which called forth His tender reproach (S. John xiv. 28 and xvi. 6, 7), was now become to them a source of joy; for on Olivet "they worshipped Him," and then, strong in the personal knowledge of His Ascension, and in the realization of their union with Him in His Ascended Life, they went back to their homes, back to the work that lay before them, back to the religious conditions under which, by GOD's Will, they lived their daily life,—"They returned to Jerusalem with great joy, and were continually in the Temple, praising and blessing GOD."

Joy in its fulness is the distinctive gift of JESUS CHRIST; it is a distinctive feature of true Christian life as lived in the Kingdom of the Incarnate. *Servite Domino in lætitia,*—"Serve the LORD with gladness," —is the very leading principle of life in the Catholic Church of CHRIST, because the highest of its privileges is the worship of "GOD manifest in the Flesh" (1 Tim. iii. 16), and worship is joy. And the secret of the

joy with which the disciples returned from Olivet
was doubtless this: they had seen the vision of the
glory of the Ascended JESUS,—a glory in which each
one had so intense and personal an interest, a vision
which brought them into a posture not of transitory
but of abiding worship, into a life of continual joy,
because a life of continual adoration of "the Lamb
as it had been slain," Who was then revealed to them
as King of kings and LORD of lords.

Now, because our King is truly GOD in assumed
humanity, the same homage is due to Him that is due
to GOD. Each LORD's Day is a great court-day, when
all loyal souls go to the palace of their King to do Him
homage; and if our churches are as the palace where
He holds His court, the whole of the ceremonial ob-
served there must be in keeping with the royal state
of Him Whom we delight to honour. We cannot
imagine any earthly sovereign giving audience to an
undisciplined herd of people unrestrained by any suit-
able ceremonial; and the higher the King the more
reverent and beautiful must be the observances wherewith He is approached. The ceremonial wherewith we
draw nigh to pay homage to our King is such as is im-
posed by His Own Will, not framed by His people of
their own imagining. Our Sovereign has revealed twice
over in what manner He wills to be worshipped; first,
through that ritual of type and symbol which was im-
posed upon His ancient people with the emphatic words
applied to every detail, "As the LORD commanded
Moses," and is referred to by the writer of the Epistle
to the Hebrews in words equally emphatic: "For,
See, saith He, that thou make all things according to

I

the pattern shewed thee in the mount" (Heb. viii.
5); and, secondly, through the revelation of Heavenly
things given us in the visions of the life and worship
of Heaven granted to S. John, and related by him in
the Apocalypse.   And through all the ages of the
Christian Church the Ascended JESUS has been thus
worshipped.

There are two orders of worship revealed to us in
the Word of GOD.   The first of these is the worship
of GOD in Himself,—that worship which was shown
in vision to Isaiah (Isa. vi. 1–4) when he heard the
glorious seraphic song since embodied in the "Ter
Sanctus" of the Church on earth; but that worship,
though it has received through the clearer revelation
of the Gospel an intensity of expression which it lacked
before CHRIST came, is yet not the distinctive feature
of the Christian Church.   Where GOD is known GOD
is worshipped, and we Christians worship GOD in Himself the more intelligently because He has revealed
to us the mystery of His Tri-Une Nature, and we
worship Him as One GOD in Trinity and Trinity in
Unity.   But the distinctive worship of the Christian
Church is the worship of the Incarnate GOD, the Man
CHRIST JESUS, Who in our nature is seated at GOD's
Right Hand, and in that nature is by us to be adored.
The Ascension Day marked a distinct crisis in the
worship of GOD both in Heaven and on earth.   Until
that mysterious morning when JESUS in His assumed
Humanity passed within the Veil and took His place
within the true Holy of Holies, the "Agnus Dei,"
the great hymn of Christendom, had never rung
through the courts of Heaven; but when the throng-

ing Angels watched the Ascent of the Sacred Humanity of JESUS,—and saw its mysterious flight cease only when it was throned on the Right Hand of the Eternal,—a new light flashed across their intellects, a new adoration filled their spirits, a new song burst from their lips, a new worship was begun, the worship of JESUS CHRIST: "Worthy is the Lamb that was slain to receive power, and riches, and wisdom, and strength, and honour, and glory, and blessing!" (Rev. v. 12). And as the Ascension of JESUS formed a crisis in the worship of Heaven, so was it also on earth. "They worshipped Him,"—His very withdrawal from among them, His very elevation to the Throne of GOD, was the development of new relations between the disciples and their LORD. As long as He was on the earth the worship of Him was not the principal feature of their life; but as soon as He was withdrawn from them and seated at GOD's Right Hand in the Heavenly places, the adoration of the Lamb,—the worship of JESUS Incarnate, Crucified, Risen, Ascended, Enthroned,—the distinctive worship of the Christian Church,—began to be. And a new aspect stood revealed of that holy Eucharist which He had ordained: it was to be the earthly centre of that glorious worship wherewith, in Heaven, in Paradise, and on earth, the Ascended JESUS is ever adored.

It is important to remember that this posture of worship towards the Incarnate, this adoration of the Lamb, is both our duty and our privilege; for it meets a difficulty that is sometimes raised against the worship of the Church. That worship is a beautiful

worship,—into its use all forms of beauty are brought—
beauty of architecture, of painting, of music and song,
of colour, of needlework,—every lovely creation of art
is by the Church called into her service as expressing
her love and adoration of her LORD. But to this it
is objected that such worship is unfitting, because the
GOD Whom we worship is pure Spirit, and they that,
worship Him must worship Him in spirit and in
truth. But, supposing us to accept the premiss, we
must deny the application, because we believe that,
even as pure Spirit, GOD is well pleased with the offering of a beautiful worship, since all beauty is His Own
creation, called into being for His Own enjoyment ;
and the Bible tells us, "The LORD shall rejoice in
His works" (Ps. civ. 31). But we cannot accept
the premiss, because ours is not the worship of One
Who is pure Spirit and that alone ; if we were to
hold that opinion we should be denying our position as Christians and allowing ourselves to drift
back into Theism. We worship GOD-made-Man,
Whom we adore not only in His Divine but in His
Human Nature ; and all that man in the highest perfection of his nature, in his most developed state,
loves and appreciates, that the One Ideal Man loves
and appreciates too. Whatever faculty is in the
creature must first be in the Creator, and the love of
the beautiful, and the power of art to gratify that love,
could not exist in man if they had not their source
and spring in the Divine Nature. The beauty of
nature is a joy to the Heart of GOD,—"He hath
made every thing beautiful in his time" (Eccles. iii.
11),—and if He rejoices in the beautiful things which

are His immediate creation, will He not take delight
in those beauties of art which are also His creation
through the medium of the mind of man,—when they
have not only an intrinsic but also a *moral* beauty
as the offering to Him of His children's adoration?
Therefore it is our belief that the worship which we
offer as Catholic Christians is acceptable to our Ascended King both in His Divine and in His Human
Nature.

Behold Him, the Ascended JESUS, enthroned at
the Right Hand of GOD! See Him there, the pleading Priest, the bountiful King, the Head of the Body,
the LORD of the Sacraments, the Guide of individual
souls, the great Minister of His Own Priesthood in
Heaven, through us His members ministering on
earth, calmly and restfully waiting in magnificent
confidence at GOD's Right Hand through all the
long and weary ages, "expecting till His enemies be
made His Footstool." Thus gazing on Him in His
loveliness and magnificence, fall low at His Feet in
whole-hearted self-surrender, and in every act of
formal worship in His Church or of private devotion
at home, and in all the consecration of your daily
life, pay Him the homage of a joyful worship, as the
Apostles did of old.

Thus live, and you shall live a life of spiritual
ascension; thus live, and in some degree Heaven
shall be known to you, not as longed for in a distant
future, but as enjoyed in the living present. For this
is Heaven (what matters the locality?)—to live in the
vision of the Ascended JESUS, to live in union with
the Enthroned LORD. Thus to go on my way is to

have my heart filled with joy; thus to go on my way
is to learn to speak the language of continual praise
and thanksgiving; thus to go on my way is to live as
my LORD would have me live in the peace and joy
of union with Him in His Catholic Church; learning
in every Eucharist,—ay, and every moment from
Eucharist to Eucharist,—"with Angels and Archangels, and all the Company of Heaven," by word
and deed "to laud and magnify His glorious Name."

"Alleluia! sing to JESUS!
  His the Sceptre, His the Throne;
Alleluia! His the triumph,
  His the victory alone.
Hark! the songs of peaceful Sion
  Thunder like a mighty flood;
JESUS out of every nation
  Hath redeemed us by His Blood.

Alleluia! not as orphans
  Are we left in sorrow now;
Alleluia! He is near us,
  Faith believes, nor questions how:
Though the cloud from sight received Him,
  When the Forty Days were o'er,
Can our hearts forget His promise,
  'I am with you evermore'?

Alleluia! Bread of Angels,
  Thou on earth our Food, our Stay;
Alleluia! here the sinful
  Flee to Thee from day to day;
Intercessor, Friend of sinners,
  Earth's Redeemer, plead for me,
Where the songs of all the sinless
  Sweep across the crystal sea.

Alleluia ! King Eternal,
  Thee the LORD of lords we own ;
Alleluia ! born of Mary,
  Earth Thy footstool, Heaven Thy Throne :
Thou within the Vail hast entered,
  Robed in flesh, our great High Priest ;
Thou on earth both Priest and Victim
  In the Eucharistic Feast.

Alleluia ! sing to JESUS !
  His the Sceptre, His the Throne :
Alleluia ! His the triumph,
  His the victory alone.
Hark ! the songs of peaceful Sion
  Thunder like a mighty flood ;
JESUS out of every nation
  Hath redeemed us by His Blood."

PRINTED BY BALLANTYNE, HANSON AND CO.
EDINBURGH AND LONDON.

www.ingramcontent.com/pod-product-compliance
Lightning Source LLC
Chambersburg PA
CBHW020751020726
47495CB00008B/2372